This book [belongs]
to:
Samantha
Calabrese

BARBARA WILLIAMS

The CRAZY
Gang Next Door

THOMAS Y. CROWELL   New York

Typography by Joyce Hopkins
1   2   3   4   5   6   7   8   9   10
First Edition

Library of Congress Cataloging-in-Publication Data
Williams, Barbara.
    The crazy gang next door / by Barbara Williams.
        p.   cm.
    Summary: When a gang of wild red-haired children, claiming to be
midgets, take over the house next door while the owner is away,
twelve-year-old Kim must figure out who they are and how to get rid
of them.
    ISBN 0-690-04868-8. — ISBN 0-690-04870-X (lib. bdg.)
    [1. Humorous stories.]   I. Title.
PZ7.W65587Cr   1990   90-1350
[Fic]—dc20   CIP
                                                          AC

For Papa Morris, Maga Elaine,
and all the Johnson, Karren, and Jensen
grandchildren

The CRAZY
Gang Next Door

1

When I get home from school, Mama is sitting at her computer, the desk top strewn with book catalogs, notepads, and two million empty gum wrappers. She's staring out the window at the blossoming cherry tree like someone just waking up from brain surgery.

"What is it, Mama? You all right?" I ask.

She turns toward me and flutters her lids. "Huh?"

"You get a bad review?" I say.

She shakes her head.

"Another book go out of print?"

"Worse," she mutters thickly.

"Well, what is it, for heck's sake?"

Mama pulls a big wad of gum from her mouth and wraps it in paper before dumping it into the wastebasket. "My editor wants me to write a book for ten- to fourteen-year-olds. In three months."

"So?" I ask.

Mama sighs. "She wants it to be funny."

"Funny has never stopped you before," I remind her. Funny, in fact, is Mama's worst fault. Somehow she has managed to take every single tragedy of my entire life and turn it into a funny book for kids.

Mom picks up the wastebasket with one hand and with the other sweeps the empty gum wrappers into it. A few fall on the carpet, but she doesn't seem to care. "It has to be a mystery, and I can't think of a single mysterious plot. Except . . . that gang next door."

"The Spikes gang!" I cry. "Of course. Write a story about the Spikes gang."

Mama lets out a windy sigh and studies the cherry tree again. "I can't. Readers would never believe it."

"Of course they would. It's true, isn't it?"

"Did the police believe it?" she argues. "Did

your father? Did your sister and her husband? Even Mrs. Overfield didn't believe it." Mama unwraps a fresh stick of Juicy Fruit, folds it into fourths, and stuffs it into her mouth.

"You don't need to tell the exact truth," I point out. Mama has a talent for not telling the exact truth in her books.

"No," she admits. "But I've been sitting here for five hours thinking about it, and there's no way to change that preposterous story into anything unpreposterous. And I'd be laughed at by every thirteen-year-old in America if I tried."

"Well, I'm almost thirteen, and I wouldn't laugh at you," I say.

"Thanks." Mama gives me a tired smile and brushes my hair behind my ear. I hate it when people muss my hair after I've just fixed it, but today, on account of how discouraged she seems, I let Mom do it.

In fact, she looks so pitiful I pull up a chair, sit down, and take one of her hands in both of mine. It feels like an ice sculpture. "You can do it," I urge. "I'll help you."

"How?" she says.

"Well, I've never read one of your stories until after it was published. But this time I'll read everything as you go along. I'll tell you how to say things. I know what kids my age will believe."

"But you already believe the story," Mama argues.

"And I'll help you tell it so other kids will believe it, too." Suddenly the whole idea seems really exciting. "We'll be a great new team," I say. "Sanders and Sanders. Like the Judds, only authors instead."

"Oh, I don't know, Kim . . ." Mama's voice trails off.

"We can do it!" I urge. "Please, Mom. It will be a best-seller."

"I don't think so—"

"I'll bet you a million dollars," I say.

"You don't have a million dollars."

"Well . . ." I hesitate, but only for an instant. "I'll bet all my allowance from now until next December."

Mom gets this Mrs. Innocent expression on her face. "You really want to do it? That badly?"

"Really," I say.

She throws her arms around me. "Okay. You win. But remember, I want to be laughed with, not laughed at."

So all you readers better believe this book. It's one hundred percent true, and Mom and I have a whole lot riding on it. Her entire career as an author.

And my allowance until next December.

2

Sooner or later you'll discover that one of the nuttiest things about this book is our next-door neighbor, Mrs. Overfield, who collects things. She collects Oriental art, exotic plants, diamonds big enough to use as marbles, hightop sneakers, husbands, and stray cats. Last summer, when this story took place, all of her husbands were dead or divorced, but Mrs. Overfield still had three cats: a Siamese named Thomas Jefferson, a black longhair named Dolley Madison, and a tabby named Harry Truman. I liked the cats okay, and I thought the hightops were really great, especially for a little old lady with blue hair. Maybe I would have liked some of the husbands, too, if I'd ever met any. But on the whole, the stuff Mrs. Overfield collected seemed creepy and useless, and I wasn't crazy about it.

Actually, a person's taste is her own business unless she expects you to carry some of it for her, right out in public. And there I was, downtown in broad daylight on a Saturday afternoon, holding Mrs. Overfield's enormous blue purse. The one made of Chinese silk brocade with the cloisonné fastener half the size of a saucer.

"I feel like an overdressed Buddha," I whispered to Mama.

"Mmm?" she said. Mama was holding up her hands, fingers spread apart, comparing Mrs. Overfield's rings that she was wearing with the jewelry in O. C. Tanner's store window.

"What if one of my friends should see me?" I muttered.

"Your friends don't window-shop at O. C. Tanner's," Mom said. "They're too busy inside the mall, cruising for boys."

That was true, of course, even if it wasn't very polite of Mama to mention it. But what if one of my friends saw me on her way to the mall? What if a *boy* saw me?

I didn't see why I should be the one to carry the purse anyway. Mrs. Overfield had given it to Mom, not me. Inside it were the keys to her house and all the instructions Mama needed to take care of Mrs. Overfield's cats and plants and gimcracks while she was in New York taking care of her granddaughter and her brand-new twin great-grandsons.

Mrs. Overfield doesn't have any family in Salt Lake, so Mom and I had driven her to the airport.

As Mom stopped her Celebrity outside the Delta terminal, she said, "You're not going to wear those diamonds in New York, are you?"

"Why not?" Mrs. Overfield asked.

"You'll be mugged. Professional New York muggers are always on the lookout for women wearing big diamonds because they carry lots of money in their purses." Mama hadn't spent ten days in New York in her entire life, but she reads a lot. She was an authority on New York muggers.

"Oh, these are my cubic zirconias," Mrs. Overfield said. "My real diamonds are home in the safe behind the Japanese print in the living room."

"But New York muggers will *think* they're

real. You've said yourself that your zirconias look just like the real diamonds in O. C. Tanner's window—that you can't tell your own real jewelry from the imitation except by the inscriptions inside the rings."

Mrs. Overfield gathered her lips into a tiny pink knot while she thought about that. "Maybe you're right. Why don't you wear these rings while I'm in New York? No one will try to mug you in Salt Lake."

She took off her three fake diamond rings and gave them to Mama. Then Mama put them on her fingers, waved good-bye, and drove straight to the ZCMI parking lot to see if she could tell the difference between Mrs. Overfield's cubic zirconias and the real five-carat diamonds in O. C. Tanner's store window.

She couldn't. "I think Mrs. Overfield's rings are just as pretty as those, don't you?" she asked me.

I sighed. Loudly. I might not have minded this comparison shopping in some dark, out-of-the-way place, but O. C. Tanner's is on South Temple Street, right next door to the ZCMI mall, where all my friends hang out. "I wouldn't carry this purse on Halloween," I complained.

"Oh, for goodness' sake, Kim, give it to me."

Mom took Mrs. Overfield's purse and put the strap over her shoulder. Immediately I decided that Mom looked even more ridiculous carrying Mrs. Overfield's purse than I did, what with her own white leather bag bobbing from the same shoulder and Mrs. Overfield's three cubic zirconias sparkling on her fingers like cherry-size suns.

Mama once again studied the window display, holding her hands this way and that while she continued her research, and I was positive that Ashlee Brinkerhoff or one of her cool friends from Bryant Junior High School would walk by and see me standing with the crazy purse-and-diamond lady. So I edged about ten feet away, pretending an overwhelming interest in the china mantel clock sitting in another O. C. Tanner's window.

I was so busy ignoring Mom that I didn't see the mugger until after he'd whizzed past me, grabbed both purses from her shoulder, and knocked her to the sidewalk. Mama just sat there on the pavement, rubbing her knee and watching him disappear. Later I asked her why she hadn't at least yelled at him, and she replied that she had been so stunned to discover that muggers operated in Salt Lake City, Utah, exactly the way they do in New York City, New York, that she couldn't think of anything to say.

I sure yelled, though. "You big ape!"

Like Mom, all the Saturday shoppers dropped their mouths open to stare, first at me and then at the guy running away, as if they couldn't quite believe what they'd just heard with their own ears and seen with their own eyes on a July afternoon, right here in our own law-abiding city.

Not me. I charged after the mugger, even though I knew I'd never catch him. He was the tallest man I'd ever seen, except maybe that basketball player Mark Eaton, and most of him was legs. *"Stop him!"* I bellowed.

He darted into the street, not caring about things like proper crosswalks or red and green traffic lights. Brakes screeched and tires skidded as motorists stopped and waited for him to cross. One friendly driver even motioned for me to continue my chase, so I did.

I waved my thanks to the motorists and then signaled more frantically to the people across the street, two young men in particular who were coming down the steps of the Old Church Office Building. They were dressed like twins in white shirts and black neckties with tidy little scripture bags suspended from straps over their

13

shoulders. *"He stole my mother's purses! Get him!"* I commanded.

The young men obeyed. They separated like Denver Broncos defensive tackles to charge the thief from two directions, but once I saw them do that, I wished I'd called to someone else instead. Standing on top of each other, those two would scarcely have been as tall as the mugger, and I had mental pictures of the big guy picking both of them up by their necks and knocking their heads together.

Size didn't stop them, though. Running furiously, they somehow lunged at the purse snatcher at the same instant, which startled the mugger so badly he stopped dead for half a second. One guy snatched Mama's white leather purse from the thief and just stood there on the sidewalk, holding the trophy above his head with both hands and grinning triumphantly. That seemed to stir his friend up, too, because the second guy took right off again to chase the giant alone—through beds of purple petunias and yellow marigolds and red salvia in the beautiful formal gardens at the side of the Old Church Office Building. The mugger strode effortlessly toward the back of the building as the second man jogged behind, his scripture case bouncing up and down from his shoulder like a rectangular yo-yo.

No luck. He returned a few minutes later, bent over at the waist and panting like a diesel truck that needed a tune-up.

By then Mom had joined the first man and me on the north side of the street.

"He jumped over a wall," the second guy explained breathlessly. "I'm sorry."

"Oh goodness," Mama wailed. "How will Mrs. Overfield's Venus's-flytraps get enough protein to eat if I don't feed them my spiders?"

The second man shuddered. Maybe from horror, maybe from all that panting. I couldn't tell. "You had spiders in that bag?" he asked.

"Goodness, no," Mama explained. "That bag came all the way from mainland China. You don't put spiders in silk-brocade bags with real cloisonné fasteners."

The two guys shared a look that was partly relief and partly befuddlement. I don't suppose they'd ever met anyone who collected weird stuff, like Mrs. Overfield.

Her own white purse tucked safely under one arm, Mama spread out her hands to study her sparkling fingers. "Well, at least he didn't get Mrs. Overfield's cubic zirconias. But I'm going to lock them up before anyone else thinks they're real diamonds." Suddenly she looked up. "Oh, I'm sorry. I haven't even thanked you boys properly for helping. I really am grateful. And I want to give you both a reward."

She opened her white purse and reached for her wallet, but the first guy took her by the arm to stop her. "Oh no, ma'am. We can't take a reward for just doing what's right. But maybe you'd like to take a few minutes to hear our first discussion about the restored Gospel."

"That's very nice of you to offer," Mama said sweetly. "But right now I've got to go to the police station so I can feed the presidents and their beautiful little girl friend."

3

Mama gets paid for writing books. But what she writes mostly are notes to herself on those big pads of lined yellow paper. She calls them "research."

Her "research notebooks" are about as interesting as the case history of a patient with constipation. And as easy to read as the doctor's prescription for the pharmacist.

Mama studied shorthand one summer when she was in high school. She never mastered the subject well enough to become a stenographer, but she remembers a few of those little curlicues that stand for whole words. And over the years she's made up a few special squiggles of her own. When she writes in a hurry, as she always does when she's setting things down in her research notebooks, she works up a fury of curlicues and squiggles, with just a few real words sprinkled here and there.

"Good research is the handmaiden of good fiction," she always says. "And good authors research every life experience that comes their way because they're bound to need the information sooner or later for a book."

So when she reached in front of me and pulled her current notebook out of the glove compartment, I knew the two of us were headed for a Life Experience.

We had just parked on Fourth South, on the north side of the Metropolitan Hall of Justice. I'd been to that square at least once a week since the time I was three months old because the library sits on the southwest corner. But Mom never had any reason to go to the courthouse or the police station or the jail. So we'd always parked near the library, away from the cars of people who had livelier business to attend to in the other buildings. The truth is that I'd never really noticed the north or east sides of the plaza before, and now the whole square seemed both novel and familiar at once, like a fresh-smelling box of crayons that's never been opened.

I guess Mama was too upset right then to notice things, because she climbed out of her side of the car, tucked her notebook and purse securely under one arm, and set off toward the police station, her forehead leading the way like the locomotive of a train. I caboosed behind, peering one way and another to study as much of the plaza as I could and still more or less keep up with her.

Suddenly one of the men who was pulling weeds from a planting area set inside the plaza looked up at me and smiled. "Hi there. Warm out today, isn't it?"

"Huh?" I said.

I couldn't remember whether it was warm out or not. I couldn't think about anything except that the man was wearing a white T-shirt with big black letters that read: SALT LAKE COUNTY JAIL.

This guy was a convict. And he was talking to *me.*

The only other criminal I'd ever ever had anything to do with acted exactly the way criminals were supposed to. He stole something (two purses) and ran. So this friendly guy with the wavy brown hair turned my vocal cords to jelly. Worse than that, he startled me so badly I tripped and fell right there on the sidewalk. In front of the entire world.

Gracefully he reached out an arm and swooped me to my feet. But Mama, who'd allowed *herself* to be knocked down earlier in the day, wasn't going to let any criminal touch *me*. She spun around and charged over to us like a mother grizzly bear.

Before she could rip the guy's arms off, I got my voice back. "Thank you," I squeaked.

Mama relaxed. "Uh—yes. Thank you, Mr. uh . . ."

"Pokorsky. P-o-k-o-r-s-k-y. Clyde L. Pokorsky."

"How do you do," Mom said. She opened her Life Experience notebook to a blank page. "Lovely garden you have here. So-o-o," she said with a hum. "Do you enjoy your work?"

I wanted to die. When Mama's doing her Life Experience research, she asks people all kinds of terrible questions. And she never even notices that I want to die.

"Oh, I can't complain," he said with another smile. "The air conditioner is broken in the jail.

It must be a hundred and fifteen degrees in there."

"Goodness. I hope they get it fixed before you have to go back."

"We'll vote for that, eh?" Mr. Pokorsky said, waving to the two other men who were pulling weeds. One of them, with dark hair, had on a jail T-shirt, too. The other man's shirt had a picture of Tina Turner.

"You know it," said the dark-haired man.

Mama made a few squiggles on the page. "So-o-o," she said. "How long have you been doing this kind of work?"

Even though I knew my face had turned purple with mortification, even though I wished I could drop through a trapdoor in the cement plaza and disappear to China, I had to admire the way Mom kept thinking up so many Life Experience questions to ask.

"Okay, wiseguys," the man in the Tina Turner shirt said gruffly. "Get back to work. The both of you." He gave them a shove, and for the first time I realized he wasn't an inmate, too. But I didn't like him. Besides the fact that you could have potted a plant with the dirt from his neck, his eyes were mean.

Mama waved toward Mr. Pokorsky. Then she

21

tucked the purse and notebook back under her arm and hiked off across the plaza, following the arrows pointing to the Complaint Desk.

There were so many arrows I was sure the Complaint Desk would have a line in front of it a million miles long. But I was wrong. No one else was there. Maybe all the complainers had heard about the air conditioner in the jail being broken and thought the police department might be a hundred and fifteen degrees, too.

It wasn't. It was cool as a canyon breeze and freshly painted, not at all like the precinct house on those *Barney Miller* re-runs. Mama stood up to talk to the desk sergeant through a little hole in a glass window, but he was sitting at a desk, in front of a computer keyboard.

Mama sounded a little breathless. "Do you know a mugger who's as tall as Larry Bird?"

"Larry Bird? The basketball player?" the sergeant asked.

"Yes," Mom said. "Nearly seven feet tall. You must know him. And where to go to arrest him."

"No, ma'am. I can't say that I do." The sergeant stood up to put a paper on another desk, and I noticed he was wearing a double holster with guns on both hips. I also noticed he wasn't as big as I had expected him to be for a man with

22

such a huge upper torso. In fact, there was something about the way his enormous head rested right on top of his shoulders that reminded me of those buffaloes you see at Yellowstone Park.

"Well, I hope someone in the police department knows how to arrest him," Mom said. "It's a matter of life or death."

He sat down again and folded his hands on the desk. "Just whose death are you worried about, ma'am?"

"Mrs. Overfield's cats!" Mama wailed, and then probably because she saw him roll his eyes at the ceiling, she slowed down to explain more calmly. "Mrs. Overfield lives in the other half of our duplex. She has three valuable cats. Thomas Jefferson and Dolley Madison and Harry Truman. And she has at least fifty exotic plants. She locked all the cats and plants in her house, and I promised I'd take care of them while she's in New York helping her granddaughter who just had twin boys. But that big bully knocked me down and ran off with the Chinese silk purse that has Mrs. Overfield's keys."

I guess the officer didn't think that Mrs. Overfield's three cats and fifty plants were worth an all-points bulletin. He didn't come right out and say that, exactly. He just said, "Was there anything of value in the purse?"

"Goodness, yes. She told me she wrote down all the instructions for taking care of the cats and plants. And her granddaughter's unlisted telephone number in New York in case I have to call her for anything. And the day of her return flight so we can go pick her up at the airport."

"I mean things like money or jewelry."

"Oh, I don't know about things like that," Mama said. "I didn't have a chance to look in the purse before that mugger stole it."

"You want to file a formal complaint?" the officer asked.

"Well, of course I want to file a formal complaint. He knocked me down and stole the purse with Mrs. Overfield's keys."

The officer cleared his throat and turned to his keyboard. "I'll need your full name and address."

"Janice B. Sanders. He stole my own purse, too, but someone rescued it. Do you need that man's name?"

"One thing at a time, ma'am. Your address, please."

He asked Mom a lot of ordinary questions like that, but Mama didn't seem to mind. While he was typing all her answers into his computer, she was scribbling down all his questions into her research notebook, in case she ever decided to write a book someday about a desk sergeant.

When he was through, Mama said, "How long do you think it will take for the police to find Mrs. Overfield's purse?"

The officer screwed up his mouth. "Well, I can't promise they'll ever find it. Our department is understaffed, you know. And we can't assign anyone to look for a purse that didn't have any valuables in it. But the thief will probably throw the purse away when he discovers there isn't anything in it worth keeping. So it's possible that someone will find it and turn it in."

Mama was outraged. "That could take weeks! Those adorable cats and all those valuable plants would be dead by then!"

The officer shrugged and turned to another complainer who was now standing behind us. "Next!"

"But—" Mama sputtered.

"Sorry, ma'am," the desk sergeant said. "Maybe you can find some other way to get into your neighbor's house."

"Hmmph," said Mama. "Maybe I can!"

She trotted right out of the police station and over to the planting area on the plaza, where Mr.

Pokorsky and the dark-haired man were kneeling side by side pulling weeds. The man in the Tina Turner shirt was sitting on a granite bench to watch.

"Do any of you gentlemen know a mugger about this tall?" Mama stretched her notebook high in the air to show them.

Mr. Pokorsky smiled. "I don't think I've had the pleasure," he said.

"Try to remember," Mom insisted. "You can't miss him. He's as tall as Larry Bird."

"Doesn't sound familiar," Mr. Pokorsky said. He turned to the dark-haired man. "You know him, Carlos?"

Carlos wiped his forehead with the back of his hand and shrugged. "Not me, man. I don't know no tall guys. Ask Miller." He nodded toward the third man, sitting on the bench. "He's the smart one knows everything. You know a tall guy, Miller?"

Miller scowled. "Maybe I do and maybe I don't. What did this dude do?"

"He knocked me down and stole Mrs. Overfield's purse with the keys to her duplex," Mama said. "She's our next-door neighbor who's going to be in New York for a while, and

I promised to take care of things while she's away. But now I can't get in to feed her cats or water her plants."

"I hope she won't be gone too long, or that kitty litter is sure going to stink!" said Miller.

"The cats will starve," Mr. Pokorsky said.

"Maybe the house is full of mice," Carlos suggested.

"Surely you must have heard someone in the ja——, in there, talking about a tall mugger," Mama said.

"I'll keep my ears open," Mr. Pokorsky promised.

"Please ask around among your friends at the jail. Someone—in there—is bound to know about a mugger who looks like a basketball player, and how I can find him to get Mrs. Overfield's keys back," Mom said.

For once the ugly look disappeared from Miller's face. "Is there a reward?"

"Well—goodness—of course!" Mama said. Then she opened her purse and got out some of those little business cards that Dad gave her for Mother's Day. They're printed in raspberry-colored ink and have three raspberry-colored stripes up the left side, and they say:

JANICE B. SANDERS
free-lance writer
1226 Federal Way
Salt Lake City, Utah 84102
(801) 555-0771

Mama gave a card to each one of the men. Then she smiled and shook hands with all of them, and we walked back toward our car.

But as soon as we were far enough away that the men couldn't hear us, I turned to her. "Do you know what you just did?"

"What?" she said.

"You just gave two convicted criminals your name and address!"

"Oh tish," Mama said.

She was so sure she'd done the right thing that I didn't even bother to tell her what my real worry was. My real worry wasn't Mr. Pokorsky or Carlos, the two inmates, but that scowling Mr. Miller with the dirty neck, greasy hair, and mean eyes.

4

On the way home from the grocery store, where Mom stopped to pick up a few things for dinner, neither one of us felt much like talking. I guessed Mama was thinking about the same thing I was— how we were going to fill a few stomachs besides our own: Thomas Jefferson's and Dolley Madison's and Harry Truman's.

As we idled at the stop sign on South Temple and University Street and were practically home, I said, "Well, now what are we going to do?"

"Start dinner, I guess," Mama said. "I wanted

to fix your dad a nice one his last night in town. He leaves for Park City at seven o'clock in the morning."

"I mean about Mrs. Overfield's cats. They could die if we don't get them some food and fresh water soon."

"I know," Mama said, shifting into first and stepping on the gas. "I've been worrying about that."

"We've got to do something," I reminded her.

"Well, the desk sergeant said we'd have to find some other way to get into Mrs. Overfield's house. So—" She gripped the steering wheel so tight her knuckles turned yellow. "We'll just have to break in."

Boy. That sounded like so much fun I was almost glad the mugger had knocked Mama down and run off with Mrs. Overfield's silk brocade purse.

Mama braked the car and turned off the ignition in front of our house because this was Dad's week to use the garage and Mom had to park on the street.

That's one of the things you should remember if you ever decide to buy a duplex, especially an old-fashioned one built a million years ago before World War II. You have to share a garage with the other occupants, and there's never enough room in it for everyone's cars. Exactly two spaces. Besides how small our garage is, it sits in a narrow little alley behind the duplex, and you can't even see it from the street.

Dad doesn't mind the alley too much, but he sure hates parking his new Honda Accord on the street for the sea gulls to drop their messages on, even if he only has to do it every other week.

"You'd think Mrs. Overfield would get rid of that old T-bird if she's never going to drive it again," Dad always complains.

"She does drive it," Mom argues.

What Mom means is that Mrs. Overfield drives her car every Saturday to Smith's Food King at Fifth Avenue and E Street for her weekly groceries. What Dad means is that a round-trip of 3.6 miles once a week hardly seems worth the insurance Mrs. Overfield has to pay on the car, not to mention the room it takes up in the garage. They both wish she'd go grocery shopping with Mom.

So do all the neighbors.

Every Saturday about ten A.M. Mrs. Overfield gets this grim look on her face and marches out the back door to the alley. She bangs the garage door up, unlocks the car, and climbs aboard the bright-yellow classic. Then, after a deep breath, she bites her tongue and turns the key in the ignition.

Sometimes the engine starts right away, but not often. Usually it wails like a tomcat in the night as Mrs. Overfield leans closer and closer to the steering wheel, her face growing red. Finally the engine noise sounds more like a purr and Mrs. Overfield shifts into reverse. *Zoom!* She's out of the garage and smashing into garbage cans all the way to the street.

You never get used to how loud the takeoff is. Or how dangerous. So parents who live on Federal Way or Butler Street and share our back alley always keep their little kids locked indoors on Saturday mornings.

Later, when Mrs. Overfield's car is safely back in the garage and no one has to worry about alley disasters for seven more days, Mom always says, "I think it's wonderful that a seventy-six-year-old woman tries so hard to stay independent."

What she really means is that she's glad Mrs. Overfield likes to walk and does a lot of it.

You have to admit that Mrs. Overfield is a good walker. She walks every day. To the beauty parlor on Tuesdays and Fridays. To the video store on Saturdays. To the university five days a week for her Spanish class. To the Unitarian

Church on Sundays. All that walking explains why she has such a world-class collection of hightop sports shoes. Real state of the art.

Mama and I got the grocery bags out of the trunk of her car and went into the house, where Dad was in his study, shuffling papers he'd need for his conference in Park City. Dad teaches art history at the university and spends most of his summers traveling around the country to art museums or conferences. There's always a two-week conference in Park City in July, and because that one is so close—just forty-five minutes away—Mom and I usually go with him. But this year we decided not to. Taking care of Mrs. Overfield's cats and plants would mean just too much commuting.

"Hi," Dad said. "Where have you been?"

"Don't ask," Mom said.

She didn't mean that, of course, and Dad knew it, because he said, "I thought you were going to take Mrs. Overfield to the airport."

"I did," Mom said.

"In your car?" Dad asked.

"Of course in my car."

"Then where's her car?"

"What do you mean where's her car?"

"Well, it isn't in the garage."

"Of course it's in the garage. It's always in the garage," Mama reminded him.

"It's always in the garage except right now."

"Don't tease. I've had a bad day."

"Well, maybe your day just got better. There's an extra parking space available in the garage. Too bad I won't be home so we can enjoy it."

"*Donald!*" Mama scolded.

"I'm serious, Janice. Go see for yourself."

Mama got this no-nonsense look on her face and turned to go out the back door. But before she got that far, I heard a claptrappy noise outside in front and saw a clunky yellow T-bird chugging up the street. "Look!" I yelled. "There it is!"

It was Mrs. Overfield's Thunderbird, all right. You don't mistake a one-of-a-kind car like that. We all watched as it sputtered to the corner and turned right on Wolcott Street.

"That's odd," said Mama.

Dad went back to sorting papers. "Oh, Mrs. Overfield probably arranged for someone to service the car while she was out of town and the mechanic is just returning it. It certainly could use a good tune-up."

"It sure doesn't sound as if it had a tune-up,"

34

I suggested.

"Yes, and why didn't the mechanic stop and come to the door?" Mom asked.

Dad waved his hand in the air as if the question weren't important. "She probably told him to put it back in the garage when he was through. He'll bring us the keys and garage door opener as soon as he's put the car away."

Mama looked more upset than she'd been all day. She turned to me. "You don't suppose Mrs. Overfield left the garage door opener in her silk brocade purse, do you, and the mugger came and stole the car?"

"How would he know where to come?" I asked. "She would have taken her driver's license and other ID with her to New York."

"Not necessarily," Mama said. "She could have left something in her purse that—"

"Like what?" I asked.

"Oh, an envelope someone sent her. Or a piece of her own stationery. Or—"

"What mugger?" Dad said.

Mama's eyes flashed. "The one who stole her purse, of course."

Dad stopped messing with the papers on his desk.

"You should have seen him," I added. "At least seven feet tall. But two little guys took after him—"

"And they got *my* purse back, at least," Mama said.

Dad sighed. "Could the two of you stop talking at once and tell me about it so I can understand you? From the very beginning?"

Mama sat down on the love seat in Dad's office. But only on the edge of the cushion. And she kept wringing her hands as she talked.

And she told Dad everything that had happened—from the time we took Mrs. Overfield to the airport until we left the square at the Metropolitan Hall of Justice.

The only thing she left out was the part that worried me the most—that she'd given her business cards to Mr. Pokorsky and Mr. Carlos and Mr. Miller.

Any of those three guys could send a message to some pal on the outside about a house that would be vacant for a while and exactly where to find it.

In the other half of the duplex at 1226 Federal Way.

5

"That mechanic didn't put Mrs. Overfield's car in our garage," I said. "He's driving up the street again right now."

"What?" Mama leaped to her feet, looked out the window, and grabbed her purse. "I'm going to follow him and find out what's going on. You two fix yourselves some dinner. There are salmon steaks and vegetables in those grocery bags."

"Wait for me!" I cried.

I raced after her to the street and climbed into the car just as she started the engine.

"Well, as long as you're here, you'd better help," Mom ordered. "Don't let that car out of your sight."

"Got you," I said.

This was going to be fun. A real car chase. Just like in the movies.

The yellow car was stalled half a block ahead of us at the intersection of Federal Way and Wolcott Street. You could hear the driver grinding gears back and forth and turning the key in the ignition over and over and making all kinds of shuddery noises.

"It certainly doesn't sound like a very good mechanic who's driving that car," Mama observed.

"It doesn't look like one either," I said.

The Thunderbird had been stopped so long at the intersection that Mom and I easily caught up with it and were now right behind, close enough to notice that the head of the driver barely extended above the steering wheel. It was a *kid* driving Mrs. Overfield's vintage automobile. A little redheaded kid.

Other curly heads kept bobbing up and down in the backseat like red popcorn so you couldn't count exactly how many kids there were all together in the car. Four maybe, or five.

"Who do you think those children are?" Mama asked.

It was one of those kinds of questions that people don't expect an answer to, so I didn't offer any. Besides, I was having a hard time figuring it out myself.

The T-bird suddenly jerked forward and then, without signaling, the driver made a sharp right onto Wolcott Street. You could tell this wasn't going to be the world's most exciting car chase. The Thunderbird was going about fifteen miles an hour as it poked along the street past the entranceway into our alley.

Mama got this do-or-die look on her face. "Hold on," she instructed me. "I'm going to pass them and stop my car right in front so they'll have to stop, too. Be prepared to jump out of your side of the car and I'll jump out of mine, and we'll run back and talk to them."

Well. That sounded more like it. I bit my lip, waiting for the action to begin.

Mama stepped on the gas, swerved out into the left lane, and raced down to the Pi Beta Phi house to stop. But we didn't exactly block the T-bird. Out the back window we saw it turn right into the second alley on the street, the one behind the fraternity houses.

"Good night!" Mama muttered as she started the Celebrity again and backed up to follow the other car.

Why had those dumb kids gone down this alley? I wondered. If they were looking for the garage where Mrs. Overfield's car belonged, they were in the wrong place.

Mama asked my question out loud. "Do you suppose they're lost?"

I shrugged. "Could be."

We followed behind the yellow dinosaur as it moseyed and dawdled down the short alley until it hit Butler and suddenly lumbered off to the right.

By now I'd realized that the driver ahead of us was not only a kid but a female kid. "Do you think the mugger threw Mrs. Overfield's purse away and that kid found it?"

"I certainly intend to find out," Mama said. "I have a whole list of questions I plan to ask that young lady."

Well. That would be a switch. Up to now the only kid Mom had ever interviewed for her Life Experience research was me. It would really take the pressure off if she'd start translating someone else's personal tragedies into "funny" books for a change.

The T-bird turned right on University Street for a few yards and then lurched right again into the long alley. Ours.

Now the real crazy pace began. Like a snail with hiccups. At every garage door on the Federal Way side of the alley the Thunderbird would come to a full stop before sputtering forward again. You had the feeling that the driver was making all those stops so she could monkey with the garage door opener in her car and see which door would open.

Sure enough, when the car stopped at our garage, the door shot up. *Bingo!* But the T-bird didn't turn into the empty space next to Dad's blue car as you'd expect. Maybe the driver was confused by the sudden appearance of that Honda Accord in the garage. Maybe she was troubled by Mom's white Celebrity so close on her tail. Anyhow, the Thunderbird just sat in the alley in back of our house while all those frizzy redheaded kids inside the car huddled and pointed and smacked each other.

Mama turned off the ignition of her car and opened the door. "I'm going to find out what's going on," she said. But as soon as she had one foot on the ground, the Thunderbird jerked forward and headed up the alley.

"Hold on!" Mom hollered, but of course the yellow car didn't. So Mama climbed back in our car and turned on the engine. We got to Wolcott Street just in time to see the yellow car turn left and race west down Federal Way about fifty miles an hour.

I rolled down my window a couple of inches. *"You dummy!"*

"That's a one-way street!" Mama added.

I don't suppose anyone heard us, except maybe Mrs. Abercrombie, who looked up from her begonia bed with a scowl. So Mama stepped on the gas and streaked toward South Temple, where it's legal to turn west, skidding around the island in the center of the street on two wheels. Whoo-ee! I guessed we were going to have one of those great car chases like the ones in the movies after all, if the featherbrained kid driving the T-bird didn't get into a three-siren accident before we caught up with her.

At the speed the car had been traveling in the wrong direction down Federal Way, anything could happen. Maybe it would jump the curb and run up on someone's lawn. Maybe it would bump into Mr. Dillingham's fire hydrant and rocket straight up into the air. Maybe we'd find it smashed to bits in one of those really gory accidents with broken glass all over and children screaming their lungs out and old ladies fainting on the sidewalk.

But by the time we reached University Street there wasn't a single yellow car or ancient Thunderbird or lunatic kid driver anywhere in sight.

You wouldn't believe a conspicuous car like Mrs. Overfield's could disappear into thin air, but it did. Mama drove around the neighborhood three times just to make sure, her face growing more and more pinched-looking and the circle around her mouth turning whiter and whiter.

Finally she pulled up to the curb in front of our house, pulled a package of Big Red gum from her purse, and offered me a stick. I didn't take one—I never do—but Mama unwrapped one for herself, folded it into fourths, and stuffed it into her mouth so she could think.

For a long time she just looked out the window, staring and chewing, staring and chewing. At last she said, "You better go in the house and fix yourself something to eat. I'm going back to the police station."

I didn't bother to point out that not everyone likes salmon as much as she and Dad do. I just said, "I want to come with you." Maybe I could talk her into stopping for burgers or pizza on the way home.

So in a few minutes the two of us were back in the police station, standing by the window with the sign that said: DESK SERGEANT.

It wasn't the same desk sergeant we'd seen before, though. This one had ears that stuck straight out on both sides like the handles on a soup bowl. He was busy punching something into his computer, so I guess Mom figured she'd save time by having the answers to his first few questions ready. She burrowed into her purse for one of those business cards printed with raspberry-colored ink.

When he looked up, she slipped the card through the little hole in his window. "I was in here earlier today to report that my neighbor's purse had been stolen. But now someone has stolen her car. I want to report that, too."

"Yeah?" said the sergeant. "You think it was the same thief?"

"Goodness no," Mama said. "The person who stole Mrs. Overfield's purse was a man about seven feet tall." She raised her arm in the air to show him. "But the person who stole her car this afternoon was a little redheaded girl who could barely see over the steering wheel."

The sergeant looked at me. "Is this your neighbor who was robbed?"

"Of course not," Mama said. "This is my daughter Kimberly. She's only twelve years old. Mrs. Overfield is seventy-six."

"I'm twelve and a half," I said, but no one cared.

"Why isn't Mrs. Overfield making the report?" the sergeant asked.

"She's in New York, so I'm taking care of her half of our duplex while she's out of town," Mom explained. "I was carrying her purse in front of O. C. Tanner's this morning when that big man mugged me. But I guess he threw the purse away and that little girl found it. She came to our garage with some other children later on, and they stole Mrs. Overfield's car."

"Yeah? What kind of a car was it?" the sergeant said.

"A 1965 Thunderbird."

The sergeant wiped his forehead with a dirty handkerchief. "Well, I wouldn't worry too much about that if I were you. The kids will probably abandon the car as soon as it runs out of gas. They usually do."

"If they don't smash it before then," I said. "That little girl is exactly the worst driver in the

45

entire United States of America. Even worse than Mrs. Overfield."

"She *was* going pretty fast," Mom said.

"Well then, a highway patrolman will probably spot her and we'll get a report even sooner."

"I certainly hope so," Mama said. "I can't help feeling that if I'd been more careful, Mrs. Overfield wouldn't have had two robberies in one day."

The sergeant fed all the information Mom gave him into his computer and then cleared his throat. "Well, thank you for coming in, ma'am. We'll do what we can to find your neighbor's purse and car."

But you had the feeling that he didn't plan to do very much. Even about that little redheaded lunatic who was headed toward Wendover like a low-flying jet.

6

Mama and I both slept through Dad's departure for Park City, which just goes to prove what an exhausting experience we'd had the day before. I, for one, had a hard time falling asleep after we got home from Little Caesar's Pizza by the university, where we had dinner. I just tossed and turned and pounded my pillow and thought about how full I was compared to how hungry Thomas Jefferson and Dolley Madison and Harry Truman must be. And when I finally got to sleep—it must have been five o'clock in the morning—I had this terrible dream about a bunch of redheaded bandits who swaggered into a Wendover casino a-hollering and a-whooping and swiping everyone else's jackpot winnings from the silver-dollar slot machines.

It was after ten A.M. before Mom came into my bedroom. "Wake up, Kim. I need your help."

"Huh?"

"I've walked around Mrs. Overfield's duplex," Mama said, "and she left her bathroom window partway open. I think I can remove the screen and pry the window far enough to climb in, but I'll need you to hold the ladder for me while I do it."

What she meant was *I* could probably remove the screen and pry the window far enough to climb in if *she'd* hold the ladder for me while I did it.

Actually, climbing that rickety ladder and prying the window open turned out to be the easiest parts of the job. It was lots harder to stop all the blood after I cut my finger on the screen and gashed my elbow on the ledge and bumped my knee on the side of the bathtub. The room and I both looked so awful, I was practically sure that I was going to need a blood transfusion. But since I knew that Mama wanted to put our ladder back in the basement, I took my time mopping myself

48

and the bathroom up. And when I was finally through playing Florence Nightingale (with about a million of Mrs. Overfield's paper guest towels from the cabinet under her basin), I decided I was probably going to live, after all. So I limped down the hall to unlock the front door for Mama.

I guess I thought the worst of my troubles were over, but I was wrong. When I got to the living room, I couldn't believe my eyes. Or nose, either. The air was so thick with smoke you could have carved your initials in it. And seated around Mrs. Overfield's teakwood coffee table— the one that came all the way from Rangoon, Burma—were four little redheaded kids playing cards.

I gasped.

The kids all leaped to their feet at once, spraying cards and pennies into the air like sparks from a Roman candle. I must have startled them as much as they startled me, but that didn't stop them from yapping all at once.

"Who the heck are you?"

"Shoot! How did you get in?"

"No one's allowed in here but us."

"Let's tie her up till she spills her guts."

Except that one of them was a girl, you had the

feeling that you were seeing four different versions of the same dirty-faced kid: mini, small, regular, and large. Besides the identical shade of red hair, they all had pointy noses, freckles as thick as quills on a porcupine, and grimy toes poking out of their drugstore thongs. And they were all smoking pipe tobacco so strong it made your eyes water. Whoo-ee.

I stuck out my chin. "I live here," I said. "What are *you* doing?"

Four mouths dropped open as four freckled faces turned to stare at each other. I don't suppose that was the answer they'd expected, and to tell the truth I was pretty amazed at it myself, even though it was almost true.

For a minute no one spoke. Then the girl nodded in my direction and winked at the biggest kid in the bunch. He planted himself in my path and squinched up his eyes. Sort of an imitation of James Cagney in one of those old black-and-white movies you see on cable TV. "You're a liar," he said through clenched teeth holding his pipe. "We were here first. So you better get out before we throw you out."

Maybe it wasn't very smart of me, but right at that moment I was sure that crazy bunch of hoodlums wouldn't try anything worse than what they'd already done. So I wasn't scared, even though there were four of them and only one of me. Besides, I had something more important on my mind. "Where are the cats? Did you feed them? They'll need water, too. Thomas Jefferson!" I called. "Dolley Madison! Harry Truman! Where are you?"

Meow!

Through the thick maze of pipe smoke I saw the cats Mama and I had been so worried about lying senseless near the Japanese screen at the far end of the room. Bits of Kitty Dinner were scattered around the floor, and I couldn't tell if the cats had eaten themselves into a stupor after finally seeing food again or if they were half dead from inhaling the stomach-turning fumes from the tobacco that those kids were smoking in their pipes.

Worried, I started toward the cats to find out, but the smallest kid rushed over to stop me. He looked about five years old, and he seemed so ridiculous holding that pipe and trying to act like Dirty Harry that I nearly laughed out loud until he kicked me in the shins. He had the strongest toes in the entire world. "Take one more step and you're dead meat," he threatened.

Cripes! So this is what Mama and I got for

trying to do a favor for Mrs. Overfield! A mugging right out in broad daylight. Useless trips to the police station. A sleepless night worrying about the presidents and Dolley. A bloody finger and elbow. A sore knee. And now my whole leg turning blue.

I figured I had a right to feel sorry for myself, and I did. I reached down to rub my leg.

Well. The girl saw me doubled over and smiled sneakily. Then she set her pipe in Mrs. Overfield's crystal candy dish, squared her shoulders, and advanced toward me like a marine sergeant. "I'll give you ten seconds to get out of here."

Despite my pain, I stood up straight so I'd have the advantage of looking down on her. She might not have been the biggest of this nutty gang, but she seemed to be the one in charge.

"I'm supposed to be here," I argued. "Mama and I are supposed to be taking care of the"— I swept my arm in a circle—"cats and plants."

The kid with concrete toes marched over. "You ain't neither."

"Shut up, Bubba Joe." The girl pushed him out of the way and turned back to me. "We're house-sitting for our aunt—uh, Aunt Gloria—while she's in New York City."

The biggest kid nodded his head. "We met her at the airport when she was leaving."

"Yeah," piped in the next-to-smallest kid. "She told us that she'd asked someone to look in on things but she'd changed her mind and wanted us to do it instead."

" 'Cause you ain't family like us," said Bubba Joe.

I didn't know how much to believe of what they'd said—probably not a single word. But how did these kids learn Mrs. Overfield's first name, which even I had heard only once or twice in my entire life? And how did they know that she was in New York City?

What I needed to do was think up a good trick question, something that would catch them off guard and help me find out who they really were. If only my mother were here right now to help me. Asking Life Experience questions was Mama's specialty.

Like the answer to a prayer, the doorbell rang. I was sure it was Mama, losing patience because I was taking so much time letting her in.

The four kids looked at each other in surprise.

Bubba Joe started toward the door, but the girl's hand shot out faster than a frog's tongue and snaggled him by the back of his shirt. "Don't open it, dummy."

The bell rang again. And again. Hard. Mama was getting mad.

We heard her turning the knob back and forth, but the door was bolted.

"It's probably the police," I suggested. "We've already told them that something suspicious is going on in this house, and they promised to come up right away and check things out." I suppose that was the biggest lie anyone had told so far, but it was worth it to see the looks of alarm on all those faces. There was a brief silence before anyone spoke.

"Shoot, I ain't ascared of no cops."

"Heck. Me neither."

"Course not. We ain't done nothing wrong."

Mama pounded the door. "Kim!" she shouted. "I know you're in there! Open up!"

I held my breath, knowing I had to unlock the door before someone stopped me. Suddenly I lunged, but the biggest guy caught me and twisted my arm behind my back, yanking me back to the coffee table so he could set down his pipe.

He whispered against my cheek, so close there was no way I could escape the smell of sour to-bacco leaves. "You try a stupid trick like that again and I'll break your arm right off."

For the first time I realized the terrible spot I was in. No matter how harmless these little kids might look, they were dangerous as rattlesnakes to tangle with, which was something I'd learned the hard way. They might even be in cahoots with someone like Miller, the awful man with the dirty neck that Mom and I had met at the plaza. But those things didn't mean I was ready to give up without at least signaling to Mama. "Help!" I yelled. "Hel——"

Oooooh! The kid twisted my arm so hard I was sure he'd told the truth about breaking it. And with his other hand he covered my mouth so tight I couldn't make a sound.

"Don't let go of her, Earl. Hear?" the girl ordered huskily. Then she whispered to me, "And if you make so much as one more peep, we'll pull off your arm and stuff it down your throat."

What good would yelling do now, anyway? How would anyone possibly save me? The door was locked. Dad was out of town. And you didn't have to be a rocket scientist to figure out that the police dispatcher wasn't going to order any SWAT team to help us out.

Even Mama wasn't bothering to ring the bell any longer.

7

Putrid isn't a strong enough word to describe the smell of the pipe tobacco those kids smoked, and Earl's hand reeked of it as he held it over my mouth. I wondered if this was the chemical warfare that *Newsweek* magazine is always warning us about. I wondered if my brain cells were dying one by one.

Then suddenly we heard a voice coming from Mrs. Overfield's bathroom. "Help! Kim! Help!"

All five of us were in the living room, and Mama was outside. So a yell from the bathroom was enough to startle anyone, especially Earl, who I'd already decided wasn't the smartest person in the room. He jumped, let out a gasp, and forgot to keep holding me. Then he turned to stare at the girl with this dumb-ox look on his face. She stared back with a frown.

Only Bubba Joe seemed more curious than surprised. He headed straight to the bathroom to see what the commotion was all about, and the rest of us followed like beads off a string.

Cripes. Mama had wormed the top part of herself through Mrs. Overfield's tiny bathroom window—the one that I'd had so much trouble crawling through—and now seemed wedged there, half in and half out. Nobody laughed, even though it isn't often that you catch a middle-aged lady right in the act of trying to break into someone else's bathroom. I wouldn't be rude enough to mention Mama's exact weight or age. But if I tell you that she can't fit into Dad's sweatshirts and that my sister Andrea is nearly old enough to be my mother, you'll get the general idea.

The girl's eyebrows suddenly looked like the McDonald's arches. "Wh—what are you doing?" she challenged.

Without batting an eye, Mama held out her hand and smiled. "Hello," she said. "I'm Janice

Sanders from next door. Mrs. Overfield asked me to take care of her cats and plants while she's out of town."

For an instant no one said anything, and Mama just hung there on the wall, like a picture spilling out of a frame.

"Oh yeah?" said the girl at last, ignoring Mama's extended hand.

"Up there?" snarled Earl.

The next-to-smallest kid elbowed his way to the front to give Mama a piece of his mind. "We don't need you. I feed the cats and plants."

Bubba Joe tugged on the girl's jeans. "I don't want that old lady in my bathroom."

Mom smiled again, a bit thinly. You could almost hear her talking to herself about psychology and how it was more likely to work on innocent little kids than big streetwise ones. She took a deep breath. "So," she said to the smallest kid, "what's your name?"

"Bubba Joe Spikes," he replied. "And I don't like old ladies watching when I'm in the bathroom."

Mama ignored that. "Hello, Bubba Joe," she said warmly. "Who are the other children?"

"Him there is Calvin. And she's DeVeda. And"—he nodded over his shoulder—"our big brother there is Earl. And all of us want you out of our bathroom."

"Well," Mama said. "I'm happy to meet all of you. Now if you'll just help me through this window so I can feed the cats—"

I took one step forward, but Earl seized my wrist and pulled me back. "You stay where you are," he said huskily. My arm still hurt from the last time he'd twisted it, so I obeyed.

Of course Mama realized what was going on, but she pretended not to. "Well, I shouldn't expect you children to try to help me. I weigh a lot more than any of you do, and I wouldn't want to fall on anyone."

It was a big drop from the window to the bottom of the tub, and Mama was going to kill herself if she managed to go through headfirst without anyone to help her. But she kept trying anyway, grunting softly.

"You go home," Bubba Joe suggested. "The other way."

"The cats has already ate," said Calvin.

"Aunt Gloria told us we should take care of everything," said DeVeda.

Mama looked shocked. "Aunt Gloria? Mrs. Overfield couldn't be your aunt! She's told me lots of times that she doesn't have any relatives in Salt Lake."

DeVeda got that sneaky look again. "Maybe we're not from Salt Lake."

"Maybe we ain't from nowhere around here," said Calvin.

"Maybe we're from Australia," offered Earl, whose accent certainly didn't sound like Crocodile Dundee's. He was standing so close to me I could feel his breath on my cheek.

DeVeda shot Earl a dark look before speaking to Mom. "Yeah, we just got in town yesterday. We were fixing to drop in on Aunt Gloria for a surprise, but she had to up and go to New York. We just accidentally bumped into her at the airport yesterday morning and she gave us the key to her house and told us not to let anyone else in."

"Especially anyone named Sanders," threatened Earl.

"So you better go now," said Bubba Joe.

I felt like telling all these Spikeses where *they* could go, but Mama just smiled. Doing Life Experience research teaches you how to stay polite with bandits like these, I guess. "Well," Mama said, "I'd like to, but I can't move one way or another. I'm stuck. Someone will have to help me."

Earl relaxed his hold on me to shrug at DeVeda. She didn't say anything, but her cheeks seemed to be getting redder.

For no reason, Thomas Jefferson sauntered into the bathroom just then and rubbed up against my leg, asking to be petted. I reached down and rubbed his back, grateful for the time to think. "Hello, Thomas Jefferson. I've missed you."

"That cat didn't miss *you*," said Bubba Joe. "Them there cats don't want you and your ma here neither. They like us better."

"They like *me*," Calvin corrected. And sure enough, Thomas Jefferson stretched himself out as if my petting bored him and walked over to Calvin for his attention. Calvin leaned down to stroke him, and I guess that should have reassured me that the kids were taking good care of the cats so I'd feel better about everything, but it didn't. "Cats always like me the best," he added.

"Do not," argued Bubba Joe. And as if to emphasize his point, he turned his pipe, which was no longer burning, upside down and banged its contents into the lap of the jade Buddha Mrs. Overfield kept on the vanity top—the jade Buddha dating all the way back to the seventeenth

61

century in China.

That did it. Mama stopped smiling. *"Stop it! You could break that!"* she shouted to Bubba Joe and then caught her breath to speak more calmly. "You children shouldn't be smoking anyway. Don't you know it isn't healthy?"

"Maybe we ain't children," said Bubba Joe.

"Maybe we're midgets," suggested Calvin.

Mama wasn't buying that silly excuse. "Mrs. Overfield doesn't approve of smoking. She never keeps ashtrays around."

"You're telling me," said Earl.

Mama's voice was about an octave higher than usual. "Mrs. Overfield will be furious when she finds out you've been smoking here."

"Who's going to tell her?" Calvin sneered.

Mama fanned the air with her hand. "No one needs to tell her. This place smells like a blast furnace. And furthermore, I saw you driving her car down this street the wrong way yesterday. About twenty miles above the speed limit and the wrong way besides. Why, you could have killed yourselves. And wrecked a perfectly good car that didn't belong to you. But the Thunderbird isn't worth anything compared to that Buddha. Why, that Buddha is a genuine seventeenth-century jade that came all the way from

China. And you treat it like some old ashtray from an amusement park. It might surprise you to know that Mrs. Overfield's collections of jade and diamonds and Japanese prints are worth a fortune!"

DeVeda suddenly brightened. "No kidding?" she said. "Earl, let's take the girl outside and all of us can help her mother go backward out the window so they can go home."

"How come?" Earl whispered.

For once DeVeda spoke sweetly. Too sweetly. "We need to talk to our neighbors and learn about all the things that are valuable in this house. So we can take good care of them."

8

"I never should have told that gang of hoodlums about Mrs. Overfield's diamonds," Mom said as we drove to the Sizzler for Sunday dinner. "The jade objects and Japanese prints are right out in plain sight, so sooner or later the kids might have figured out how valuable they are. But I didn't need to say anything about diamonds. That awful DeVeda and her brothers are bound to turn the house upside down looking for diamonds."

"You told them Mrs. Overfield took the diamonds to New York," I pointed out.

"They didn't believe me. I could tell they didn't believe me."

"Well, they'll never find the diamonds," I argued. "Mrs. Overfield put them in her safe. And the safe is hidden behind—"

Suddenly I thought of something awful. And I could tell by the look on her face that Mama had thought of it, too. The safe was hidden behind a *Japanese print*. And if those kids decided to get nosy, the Japanese prints would be the first things they'd head for.

"Well, even if they do find the safe," I said, "they'll never be able to open it."

Mama sighed. "Two days ago I probably would have said that. Two days ago I would have said no bunch of children could ever take over Mrs. Overfield's house and car from right under my own nose. But after what's happened, nothing would surprise me now. That Earl could be a professional safe opener for all I know. And the whole lot of them could be jewel thieves on the FBI's list of ten most wanted criminals."

I could tell how upset Mama was, so I tried to think of something to comfort her. "On the other hand, maybe the Spikeses really *are* Mrs. Overfield's relatives and she really did invite them to stay in her house."

"Oh tish."

I'd run out of comforting things to say, so we drove a long time in silence, the rest of the way to the Sizzler at Ninth East and Fort Union Boulevard. Dad isn't crazy about eating out, but Mom and I love to, especially at the Sizzler. So whenever he leaves town we take turns eating dinner at all the Sizzlers around the valley. Normally I really look forward to the great salad bars and all that good Mexican stuff they have, but by the time Mama turned left onto Ninth East I'd just about lost my appetite.

"Do you think the Spikeses might really be midgets?" I asked Mom as I opened the car door.

"Of course not," Mama said. "They just said that so I wouldn't tell them to stop smoking."

"But they don't seem to have any parents or other grown-ups with them. Normal kids don't live by themselves."

"Those kids are hardly normal."

"Yeah," I agreed with a nod. "Well, *maybe* they're midgets."

"I doubt it," Mama said. "Midgets don't look like children. Those Spikeses don't act like normal children, but they look like them. I'd say Bubba Joe is probably about five and Earl is maybe a year older than you. Calvin and

DeVeda are somewhere in between."

"I can't believe people would say they're midgets when they're really not," I said.

Mama sighed. "Well, don't expect me to explain it. I can't figure any of it out."

Later, when we made our weekly phone call to Boston to talk to my sister and her husband, Andrea couldn't figure any of it out either. In fact, she couldn't believe any of it—not about Mrs. Overfield's purse being stolen by a mugger who looked like a professional basketball player or about a bunch of kids racing Mrs. Overfield's yellow Thunderbird all over town or about a troop of redheaded gangsters moving themselves into the other half of our duplex.

"Hey, Mom. Who are you trying to kid? This is me, Andrea. I know that stuff didn't really happen. I know you're just testing out the plot for a new book on me. But I hope you won't waste your time writing it and trying to get it published, because it won't fly. An editor would lose her credibility with the marketing department and the chief financial officer and every single stockholder of the company if she tried to publish anything that off-the-wall."

My sister, the yuppie.

Mama sighed. "I was afraid you wouldn't believe it. No one else does."

"Listen, Mom," Andrea said. "Have you been to your doctor for a checkup lately? I don't mean to imply you're getting delusional or anything. But maybe you've got a chemical imbalance that—"

"Well, I believe it," I argued from the other extension. "The trouble with MBA students at Harvard is that they have no imagination. They can't think in anything but dollar signs."

"Maybe not, but you should see us laugh all the way to the bank."

That isn't exactly true. Andrea and Mike aren't going to any banks lately. Ever since they gave up their government jobs in Washington to go to graduate school, they can hardly afford to rent movies for their VCR, and they live in a crummy apartment in Cambridge with a bathtub exactly a million years old that rests on legs. But all they ever talk about is the starting salaries at this "Big Eight accounting firm" or that "Fortune 500 company." You can really get depressed talking to people like that.

"Oh, I don't know, Andrea," said Mike, who'd been listening on a second phone in their apartment. "Your mom's plot might work. She writes for kids, remember, not graduate students at

Harvard. Only—"

"Only what?" I said. I guess I sounded a little mad, mainly because I was.

"There's one major flaw in it, which readers would spot right away," said Mike. "No responsible woman would allow a bunch of unsupervised children to live next door, incorrigible or otherwise. She'd report them to the child welfare authorities first thing."

"Of course. Why didn't I think of that?" Mama said. "Thanks, Mike." And she hung up.

Next thing you knew, Mama had the phone book spread out in front of her and was looking for the number of the right agency of the Utah Department of Social Services to call. Sure enough, the Child Abuse and Neglect Division had a twenty-four-hour hot line, and she dialed the number. Someone named Irwin answered.

Unlike the desk sergeant, or Dad, or Andrea, or even Mike, Irwin believed what Mama told him and listened to every word. Then he took down Mrs. Overfield's address and our address and Mama's name and phone number and promised to get someone on the case as soon as possible. Of course, this was Sunday and the division was understaffed, so things might take a little longer than usual.

Within fifteen minutes the doorbell rang.

The lady standing outside introduced herself as Ms. Jasmine Freymuller from the Child Abuse and Neglect Division. She needed to get as complete a report as possible from the complaining witness before taking any action and asked if she could come in. "You understand?" she said.

Mama understood and invited her in.

Ms. Jasmine Freymuller wasn't at all what you'd expect. I've always had this mental picture of social workers as being middle-aged ladies wearing tweed skirts and sensible shoes and men's wristwatches. Ms. Freymuller looked about half as old as my sister Andrea. She wore a cotton sundress with skimpy little straps over her shoulders, and her long brown hair was pulled back into a French braid. And she teetered so awkwardly on her high-heeled sandals that you'd swear she'd never owned a pair of grown-up shoes before.

Before they sat down, Mom offered her some lemonade, but Ms. Freymuller didn't care for any. It was important that she get straight to work, she said. Then she took a seat on one of our white leather sofas and pulled a big pile of forms from her briefcase and began asking questions.

This seemed like a good time for Mom to get

out her research notebook and a felt-tip pen, so she did. Soon she was making squiggles and curlicues on the pages the way I used to write in the sky with my sparklers on a Fourth of July night. I suppose Mama figured it would be important to know all about social workers in case she ever decided to write a "serious" book someday. "Serious" books are heavy stories about terrible things like cancer and war and alcoholism and schizophrenia and kids who hate their parents, so they nearly always have social workers in them.

"Would you mind telling me what you're doing?" Ms. Freymuller asked.

"Oh, I'm just taking my own notes on this interview. Do you mind?"

"Yes, I do mind. This is my first assignment, and it's very important I do everything right. It makes me nervous to have you writing, too."

"I'm sorry," Mama said, and put her pen down.

There were so many forms to fill out and so many questions to ask (Mama didn't know the answers to most of them, but she did her best) that the interview seemed to last about ten years. And even then it wasn't over. When she'd stopped asking questions, Ms. Freymuller

71

started rereading her notes silently to herself. First she'd read a little bit, then she'd close her eyes and move her lips, as if she were trying to memorize the entire Constitution of the United States in just one sitting. Finally she put the papers back in her briefcase and snapped the case shut.

"You've been very helpful," Ms. Freymuller said. "I'm going next door now to make some observations of my own. Our office will report back to you as soon as we've taken some action." Then she held out her hand for Mama to shake.

Mom shut the door behind the social worker and smiled at me. "Well, I guess our troubles are over."

But Mama was wrong.

Within ten minutes our doorbell rang again. Hard.

Ms. Jasmine Freymuller was standing outside again, but it wasn't the same Ms. Jasmine Freymuller we'd seen before. This one's dress was dirty and torn, her French braid was pulled apart, and one heel was broken off her brand-new pair of grown-up sandals. She was also screaming.

"You told me they were children!" Ms. Freymuller shrieked. *"Do you know that all four of*

them were smoking pipes?"

Mrs. Abercrombie looked up from her bed of begonias across the street. Mrs. Abercrombie is deaf, but I'm sure she heard every word of that.

"I didn't say they were well-behaved children," Mama said softly.

"They aren't any kind of children. I went to school twelve months a year for five years because I love all children and wanted to become a social worker and help little ones who are abandoned and mistreated. But those Spikeses are mean, cruel, ruthless, despicable *midgets!*" She spat out the last word as if it were a crime to be short, which of course it isn't.

"Oh, I know they say they're midgets," Mama said. "But they're certainly not. Little Bubba Joe couldn't be more than five years old."

"Five years old!" screamed Ms. Freymuller. "Could a five-year-old tackle me to the ground? Could a five-year-old break the heel off my shoe? Could a five-year-old kick my shins so hard I may need crutches?"

"I'm sorry—" Mama began.

"Sorry? Do you think *sorry* helps? Thanks to you, I'll be fired after my first day of work. I've just wasted the five best years of my life. But they can't fire me, because I quit." And she opened her briefcase, grabbed a handful of papers, and threw them at Mama.

Well. So much for getting any help for Mrs. Overfield's collections from Ms. Jasmine Freymuller.

9

Mama couldn't bring herself to call the Department of Social Services again, even though she knew she probably should, for fear they'd send out someone else like Ms. Freymuller and the same thing would happen all over again.

So mostly we just worried—about Mrs. Overfield's Oriental jade and Japanese prints and mega-carat diamonds. Not to mention Thomas Jefferson and Harry Truman and Dolley Madison and all those exotic plants that were probably dying of malnutrition and smoke inhalation.

Our house was so quiet you could hear the

plants growing. And I didn't have one single solitary thing to do, because Jannalee and Brynne were both at summer camp and Darci had gone to San Diego with her parents and I'd read every interesting-looking book in the whole house at least twice.

Things were so awful it was actually exciting when Mimi Saltzgiver telephoned on Wednesday, even though Mimi never calls me unless all our other friends are out of town and she has something on her mind that she's just dying to brag about to someone.

"Guess what my mother and I did yesterday?" Mimi gushed.

"I give up."

"We went shopping for school clothes and spent six hundred and twelve dollars and forty-nine cents. Like, it was un-*real*."

Six hundred and twelve dollars would be a fortune for an art history professor at the University of Utah like my dad to spend on school clothes for a kid. And Mom's income from her books—what there is of it—always winds up in Massachusetts with Andrea and Mike. "School clothes?" I said, trying to keep the envy out of my voice. Both of Mimi's parents are lawyers, and she's an only child. "It isn't even August yet.

76

Aren't you afraid everything will be out of style before September?"

"You nerd! Like Nordstrom's and ZCMI haven't stocked up on the latest fall fashions! Want to come over and see everything?"

"Well—I don't know if I should leave my mom. She's got a lot on her mind, and Dad's out of town."

"I'll let you try everything on," Mimi urged.

"I don't know. . . . My mom's really had a bad week."

"Maybe I'll even let you borrow some of the stuff. Like after I've worn it, of course."

I was pretty sure I wouldn't want to borrow much of Mimi's stuff. Her taste runs to things like oversized hair ribbons and lace shoelaces and purple sweaters with sequins, and you can never tell if she's trying to look like Cher or a Cabbage Patch doll. But I was sure if I had to spend another five minutes watching those soap operas on television, I'd start foaming at the mouth. So I told Mom where I was going and headed up the hill to the Saltzgivers' big house on Arlington Drive.

The truth is it turned out to be kind of fun trying on all Mimi's crazy outfits—a bit like getting ready for Halloween—and for the first time since Saturday I actually laughed and joked. And for about half an hour I forgot to worry about who was living next door to me and if they might be stuffing leaves from Mrs. Overfield's exotic plants into their pipes to smoke them or teaching her cats to lick all the dirty dishes instead of putting them in the dishwasher or blasting the wall of her living room to get to the diamonds inside her safe.

But then—after I'd picked out my favorite outfits to borrow someday and Mimi had promised I could—we ran out of things to talk about, and the old worries started nibbling at the side of my brain like a grasshopper chewing away at the edges of the perfectly smooth leaves in a privet hedge.

I decided to ask Mimi the question that was on my mind. Even though she talks like a foamhead some of the time, and even though I get tired of hearing about how rich she is, Mimi is pretty smart about some things. She was the only kid in my Spanish class last year who got A pluses on her tests, and she has a 4.0 average overall.

"Have you ever seen a midget?" I said.

"A what?"

"A midget."

"You mean like Billy Barty?"

"No. Not in movies or on television," I said. "I mean have you ever seen a midget in real life? Up close?"

"My Aunt Carolyn used to live next door to a lady who was pretty unreal. About four feet two. But we were never supposed to call her a midget to her face. Like, she didn't know who she was so we weren't supposed to tell her."

"If you saw someone who was really short, would you be able to tell for sure if he was a midget or a kid?"

"Of course. Wouldn't you?"

"I don't know," I admitted.

Then I told Mimi about everything that had happened from Saturday when the mugger ran off with both the purses Mom was carrying until the kids or midgets or whoever they were moved into Mrs. Overfield's house and wouldn't even let Mama and me feed her cats and plants.

"You're lucky!" she said.

"Lucky?" I repeated. Did she really think I was enjoying this crazy mess?

"I'd love to live in a little duplex with interesting neighbors like yours," Mimi gushed. "Everyone on Arlington Drive is so upper middle class and conventional. Like, it's really boring around here."

I decided to ignore the crack about my social status, mainly because the rest of what Mimi said was also true. "Why don't you come over to my house after dinner and spend the night?" I said. "Maybe we can figure out some way for you to get a good look at the Spikeses to see if they're really midgets."

"Un-*real!*" Mimi exclaimed.

"Let me call my mom to make sure it's okay," I said, "and then you can ask your mother."

"I feel just like a lady private eye on television," Mimi said. "Maybe I should wear my cranberry dress. It's so sophisticated. Just the sort of thing one of them would wear to a New York nightclub."

"Why don't you wear some shorts and an old T-shirt? We'll probably make fudge or vinegar taffy. And don't forget your sleeping bag."

"Well—okay," she said. "Oh, this is going to be so much fun!"

10

"Oh cripes!" I said. "We're out of vinegar."

"Fabulous!" said Mimi.

"What do you mean, *fabulous*? You said fudge gives you zits. You said you wanted to make vinegar taffy."

"Don't you see? We'll have to borrow some." Mimi nodded toward Mrs. Overfield's half of the duplex. "From *the Spikeses*. We'll go next door together, and I can size them up for you and tell you if they're really midgets or kids. Like, this is so perfect it's un-*real*!"

"I don't know," I said. I was remembering

Bubba Joe's steel toes and the way Earl had twisted my arm exactly four hundred degrees. "I don't think that's a very good idea—"

But Mimi wasn't listening. She grabbed Mama's Pyrex measuring cup and headed outside our door and toward the one on the west. I followed less enthusiastically. I hadn't even reached Mrs. Overfield's porch when Mimi rang the bell.

The door opened. "Who are you?" asked Bubba Joe.

"Uh—I'm Mimi Saltzgiver, a friend of Kim's." Mimi pointed toward me with an elbow. "We wonder if we can please borrow some vinegar."

"No."

Mimi's chin dropped.

"Go home," Bubba Joe added.

The door started to shut, but Mimi put her foot out so it couldn't. "Don't you want to know what we want vinegar for?" she asked.

"No," said Bubba Joe.

"We're going to make taffy." Mimi licked her lips to tempt him. "We'll give you some. Don't you want some vinegar taffy?"

By then I had climbed the steps of the porch and edged to the far side, willing to offer moral support if not brave enough to risk my shins.

"We make terrific taffy," I said. "You'll love it."

Bubba Joe scowled.

"Who's there?" called Calvin from another room.

"No one," Bubba Joe called back. To us he said, "Go home. Calvin and me isn't supposed to talk to no one."

Calvin and him? Was there a chance that DeVeda and Earl weren't home? The possibility that I wouldn't have to deal with that Ma Barker of a DeVeda or her iron-muscled bodyguard filled me with hope.

"Aren't DeVeda and Earl here?" I asked.

"They had to meet a man," said Bubba Joe.

"We only need half a cup of vinegar," I said.

"We don't got none," said Bubba Joe.

"How do you know?" said Mimi. "You haven't even looked."

"I just know," said Bubba Joe.

"Sure you have some," I said. "Your Aunt Gloria always keeps vinegar in the house. She says it's the only thing she ever mops her floors with."

That was a lie, of course. Just because Mama always used vinegar water to mop her parquet floors didn't mean that Mrs. Overfield used it on her tile.

"We'll help you find it," I added, pushing the door wider so Mimi and I could force our way in.

"And if we do, we'll give you some vinegar taffy," Mimi said.

"*Cal-vin!*" Bubba Joe yelled.

At the sound of his name, Calvin strode into the front hall where Mimi and I were now standing. He was carrying all three cats, and I have to admit that surprised me. Thomas Jefferson loved to be petted and carried. And Dolley Madison would put up with stroking once in a while. But Harry Truman thought people were a nuisance—even Mrs. Overfield—and would stalk off to attend to more important matters whenever anyone tried to touch him.

"Hi," Calvin said. "You want to see what great cats these are? I'm teaching them to bring me my pipe."

I rolled my eyes at Mimi. Of course Calvin couldn't train them to carry his pipe. Any fool knew it was impossible to teach cats to do anything, especially Harry Truman.

"Cats aren't like dogs," Mimi said. "You can't train them."

"Oh yeah? Want to see?" He set the three of them on the floor and pointed toward Mrs. Overfield's bedroom. "Okay, Blackie. Okay, Stripes.

Okay, Blue Eyes. Get my pipe."

Harry Truman sauntered off to the Japanese screen in the living room and hid behind it. Dolley Madison stretched slowly and then wedged herself under the sofa. Thomas Jefferson stayed right where Calvin had put him, on the floor in the front hall.

"Him here is the easiest to train. He's learning the fastest," Calvin explained. Then he turned to Thomas Jefferson. "Go on, Blue Eyes. Go get my pipe."

Thomas Jefferson swished his tail, looking bored.

I have to admit I thought that was pretty funny, but I was careful not to smile so Calvin could see. "Maybe you could train them easier if you called them by the right names. He's Thomas Jefferson. And the striped cat is Harry Truman. And the black one is Dolley Madison. She's a female."

Calvin reacted to that biology lesson with a scowl. "I know what a girl is," he told me. "Go on, Thomas Jefferson. Do what I showed you."

"Yeah," said Bubba Joe. "Get his pipe before I kick you."

"You won't neither kick him," Calvin ordered. "Them there cats is mine."

Bubba Joe stuck out his tongue.

"You better not stick out your tongue near those plants over there," I said, pointing to the ones in the mini-sized greenhouse at the far end of Mrs. Overfield's living room. "They might eat it."

"Huh?"

"No kidding," I said. "Those are Venus's-flytraps. They eat meat."

"Huh?" said Bubba Joe.

"You're lying," said Calvin.

"Un-*real*," said Mimi.

"Here, I'll show you if you'll find me a beetle or a spider," I said.

Calvin and Bubba Joe grinned at each other like a couple of ghouls. Then all at once Bubba Joe headed for the door.

"Don't go outside!" Calvin warned. "You know what DeVeda said she'd do if we went outside."

Bubba Joe seemed torn.

"Let's look around on all the windowsills for a dead fly or something," suggested Calvin.

"Venus's-flytraps won't eat dead bugs," I argued. "They can tell if a bug is dead by whether or not it moves. If you can't go outside, I guess I won't be able to show you how those plants eat meat." I was stalling for time, of course. I wanted a chance to look around Mrs. Overfield's house to see if the Spikeses had done anything to her valuables. And maybe Mimi needed more time to study the boys to decide whether or not they were midgets, even though I was beginning to be pretty sure that they were just rotten kids. We had to make Bubba Joe and Calvin think about something besides getting rid of Mimi and me. I winked at her.

Mimi caught my message. "Maybe there are some bugs in the basement," she told the boys. "Let's go see."

The others charged toward the stairs, and I walked straight to the framed Japanese print in the living room, the one that hid Mrs. Overfield's safe. I had the feeling that it was tipped a little bit—that someone might have been monkeying with it—but I didn't have time to study it carefully because they all pounded up the stairs. Bubba Joe was in the lead, holding his cupped hands together and shrieking like a police siren.

"I found one! I found one!"

Bubba Joe cracked open his hands to give me the trophy. "Here."

I bent over to study the gray spider but didn't reach for it. Actually, the truth is that even though I'm not afraid to touch spiders, I'm not crazy about doing it, either. "Hey, that's great, Bubba Joe. You found it, so you get to be the one who feeds it to the plant."

We all crowded around one of the Venus's-flytraps on the shelf while I explained what to do. "See those two leaves that are joined together sort of like butterfly wings?"

"Uh-huh."

"See the three hairs inside the leaves?"

"Uh-huh."

"Be careful not to touch the plant. Just drop the spider on one of the hairs."

Bubba Joe did what he was told. The flytrap snapped shut.

"Wow!" he said. "Now what happens?"

"The leaves stay shut until the spider is digested," I said.

"You kidding?" said Calvin.

Bubba Joe's eyes blazed. "Until the meat is all gone?"

"That's right," I said.

"Awesome! I want to do it," said Calvin, heading toward the basement stairs.

Bubba Joe raced after him and slugged him on the back. "Out of the way, dummy. All the bugs in the basement is mine!"

"Is not."

"Is too."

"Just try to stop me," Calvin said. And both boys thumped down the stairs.

When they were out of hearing, Mimi whispered to me. "What's that, like, garbage smell in here?"

"Tobacco. Some really weird brand."

"Tobacco? Un-*real*. I thought Calvin was talking about a bubble pipe. He's too young to smoke."

"That's what Mama told them. So then they told her they were midgets. Do you think they are?"

"They sure don't act like my Aunt Carolyn's neighbor. And they sure don't look like any midget actors I've seen in the movies. But on the other hand . . ." Mimi's voice dropped off.

"On the other hand what?"

Mimi put her finger to her lips, motioning me to be still. "What's that noise?" she asked.

There was a car out in back. A loud, tinny-sounding car. And then we heard the sound of the garage door banging open.

"Oh gosh," I whispered. "DeVeda and Earl are back. We've got to get out of here."

11

Mimi must not have been too worried about zits, because she ate nearly half the batch of fudge before we got undressed. For a girl who's five feet eight if she's an inch and has the shape of two pencils standing on top of each other, Mimi eats like a moose.

Then we packed up the rest of the fudge and a bag of Doritos and a bowl of salsa and two Diet Cokes and our sleeping bags to spend the night out in back under the stars. Mama worries when I want to sleep outdoors, but she'd long since gone to bed, and I figured what she didn't know wouldn't hurt her.

I spread out my sleeping bag and climbed into it, studying the Big Dipper while I chewed another piece of fudge. "You never finished telling me about the other hand," I reminded Mimi.

"Huh?"

"You know. I asked you if you thought the Spikeses were midgets, and you said no, but then you started to say something else."

"Oh yeah," she said. "Well, when we were talking I suddenly remembered this old movie we rented a couple of weeks ago. *Paper Moon.* Have you seen it?"

"Yeah, but it doesn't have anything to do with midgets."

"No, but it has this little girl—Tatum O'Neal when she was just a kid—who's, like, a real con artist. She smokes and everything."

"So?"

"So I don't think the Spikeses are midgets. I think they're actors."

"Actors?"

"Think about it." Mimi sat up in her sleeping bag. You could tell she was really excited about this dumb theory of hers. "What would Dustin Hoffman do if he had to play the part of an eight-year-old brat who smokes a smelly pipe and breaks into an old lady's house to live there? He'd start smoking a smelly pipe and he'd break into some old lady's house and live there. I bet the Spikeses are, like, getting into the mood for some play or movie. They might even be famous actors that we'll read about someday."

I rubbed my leg. "I wouldn't be surprised to read about Bubba Joe's toes in the *Guinness Book of Records.* I bet he could knock down the Washington Monument with his bare feet."

Suddenly Mimi put her finger to her lips for the second time that day. "Shhh."

"What's the matter?" I whispered.

"Over there," she whispered back, pointing. "A flashlight."

Sure enough, beyond the row of tams junipers that separated our half of the backyard from Mrs. Overfield's, a circle of light was bouncing around on the grass.

"What do you think they're doing?" Mimi asked.

A whole list of grisly thoughts passed through my mind, all too horrible to mention out loud: Earl hiding the cache of diamonds he'd found in Mrs. Overfield's safe; DeVeda digging up Mrs. Overfield's entire backyard to look for a secret room full of treasure; Calvin burying a poor cat who had swallowed some of that eye-watering tobacco; Bubba Joe hiding an antique jade Buddha that he'd "accidentally" kicked and broken. The possibilities sent cold chills down your back.

I snaked out of my sleeping bag and crawled over to the junipers to look through the branches. "There's only one person," I whispered. "Whoever it is, is alone."

By now Mimi was beside me on her hands and knees. "Maybe and maybe not. There could be someone else in the shadows."

Even so, I sensed it was important to act. "I don't think so," I said, sounding more brave than I felt. "The person holding the flashlight seems pretty small. Either Calvin or Bubba Joe. Will you help me grab him?" I asked her.

"Un-*real!*" Mimi cried.

"We'll crawl through to the other side of the junipers," I instructed, "one at a time so we won't make too much noise. Then we'll sneak up about ten feet. When I give the signal we'll rush him. I'll grab for the hand with the flashlight so I can shine it in his eyes and blind him. You grab the other hand and hold it behind his back." I held my breath an instant. "Ready?"

"Ready," Mimi said.

I'm allergic to junipers, and I was sure my legs

would be covered with red welts in the morning after walking barefoot through them, but it didn't matter. Nothing mattered except saving my family's honor by protecting all Mrs. Overfield's valuable possessions, as Mom and I had promised we would. I stood up slowly and tiptoed through the bushes.

Mimi followed. When we were both safely on the other side, we crept quietly a few more feet.

"Now," I whispered.

We charged.

Someone's legs began kicking in all directions.

"Ow!" I yelled. As I balanced on one foot, rubbing my sore leg against my good one, I found myself wishing a very mean thought. I found myself wishing that if someone had to kick someone, it should have been Mimi who got kicked. I'd already had my turn with Bubba Joe's iron feet, and Mimi was the one who believed she was so much bigger and stronger than all the Spikeses.

"Hey you!" yelled Bubba Joe. "Get that light out of my eyes."

"Not until you stop kicking," I said.

Bubba Joe stopped kicking, but his voice was as angry as ever.

"What the heck do you think you're doing?"

he demanded.

"What the heck are *you* doing?" I replied.

"Nothing," said Bubba Joe.

"Don't you know we're your friends, Bubba Joe? How would you like some fudge?" Mimi asked.

You had to admire Mimi for thinking to bring a bribe with her. She reached into the pocket of her nightgown and pulled out a piece of candy wrapped in wax paper.

Bubba Joe unwrapped the fudge and tossed it into his mouth. He didn't actually say thank you or anything, but you could feel his whole attitude sweetening up.

Then Mimi spoke in a voice so sweet it was almost sickening. "We were worried when we saw you out here by yourself. We thought you might be in some kind of trouble. Want to tell us about it?"

"No."

"Sure you do," Mimi encouraged. "What were you doing out here all by yourself in the middle of the night?"

"None of your business."

"Were you doing something you didn't want Calvin to know about?" I asked. I have no idea why I thought to say that. Inspiration, I guess.

"He thinks he owns all the bugs in the house. He thinks he gets to feed all the cats and them there plants, too. But I know something he doesn't know. Want to see?"

"Yes," said Mimi.

Bubba Joe put his hand in his pocket and then reached out to give something to Mimi.

"*Yeow!*" she cried. "*Worms! Take them back!*" Mimi danced and howled and practically threw them at him. I'll admit I couldn't help smiling about that just a little.

Bubba Joe grabbed the flashlight from me and shined it on his handful of squirmy mush. "Ain't they great?" he said to me as Mimi wiped off her hands on the grass. "I bet old Calvin can't dig for good worms like these."

"Uh—what do you want worms for?" I asked.

"To feed the plants, dummy. I'm going to cut them into little pieces and feed them to the plants. Worms still wiggle when you cut them into pieces."

I felt the taste of fudge rising to my mouth and was sure I was going to be sick.

"I don't think you want to do that. Worms aren't good for those plants." I didn't know whether that was true or not, but it might have been. "Anyway"—I hurried on, just as if I were

96

that man from the agricultural college's extension service who tells you on television how to take care of your grass and cherry trees—"you shouldn't give them too much meat. Each leaf dies after it's digested two or three insects and the plant has to grow another leaf to replace it. If Venus's-flytraps get too much meat, the whole plant withers up and dies."

There was something about Bubba Joe's tone of voice that made you shudder. "No one can get too much meat," he said. Then he turned on his heels and headed indoors.

My first worry was that Bubba Joe might have plans to eat Mrs. Overfield's precious cats.

But then I thought of something far, far worse.

What if I was living next door to a tribe of cannibals?

12

First thing Thursday morning Mimi's mother telephoned to say that they'd decided to go to Lake Powell for the weekend and Mimi should come straight home and pack. For two years I'd been hearing about the Saltzgivers' fabulous boat that cost $65,000 and slept eight adults and had a full-size refrigerator, but I'd never been invited to ride in it, so I was in no position to say whether anything that wonderful really existed or not. Right away I started thinking that this would be a great opportunity for Mimi to prove that it did, but somehow the idea didn't occur to her. Just as well. I don't suppose I actually would have gone off and left Mama, even to go to Lake Powell.

Mimi was dressed and out the door before I could remind her that we'd planned to go to the police station together. And I was sure she wouldn't want to do it when she got back to town the next week. Everyone knows that Mimi Saltzgiver has a very short enthusiasm span.

Besides, if Mama couldn't persuade the police department to come check things out next door, I was sure that no one could. So the truth is that I really wanted to go to the police station with her, not Mimi. But when I suggested that idea to Mama, she seemed pretty discouraged about trying to convince any desk sergeants that Mrs. Overfield's house was in a state of Red Alert emergency. She'd tried that approach more than once already, and no one had believed her. So for the time being she was practicing Creative Search—to try to remember the name and telephone number of Mrs. Overfield's granddaughter in New York.

Creative Search is something Mom learned about at a writers' conference a long time ago, and as close as I can figure out, it's something like self-hypnosis. You get a pencil and paper for doodling, and you stare out into space, and sooner or later ideas start jumping around inside your head.

Mama adds her own twist to Creative Search. She chews a big wad of gum at the same time. I know it sounds crazy, but Mama really believes in Creative Search. And she wouldn't believe in anything that didn't work.

So when she unwrapped five sticks of spearmint gum and popped them into her mouth and turned her head toward the window like someone practically in a coma, I tiptoed out of her study and went to my own room. But there was nothing to do except watch dumb game shows on television—so that's what I did.

I'd watched all of *The Price Is Right* and had switched channels for *Sale of the Century* when I heard pans banging around in the kitchen and figured I'd better go see what the newest crisis was all about.

"My cholesterol level must be too high," Mama announced when I walked in the door.

"Huh?"

"I must need some oat bran. I haven't had any oat bran for three days."

"Huh?"

"It didn't work," Mama said. "Creative Search

never works when I don't eat properly and let my cholesterol level get too high. I haven't had any oat bran for three days. When I stared out the window, all I could see was robins eating those wormy cherries that your father didn't spray properly."

"Hah! Andrea was right! You *do* have a chemical imbalance!" I thought that joke might cheer her up, but it didn't.

She sighed. "Thanks a lot. Nothing like having both your children decide you're ready for the loony bin. Plus the entire Salt Lake City Police Department. Not to mention a social worker young enough to be your granddaughter."

"I'm sorry," I said. I really was. "Can I make you some hot oat bran cereal?"

"Thanks. That's sweet of you. But I'm afraid I'd gag on that stuff right now. It's bad enough in the winter when I'm hungry. Besides, when you eat it straight, it sticks to your teeth." She opened another cupboard door. "I'm going to make some oat bran muffins."

"Oh, they're good. Make some extra ones for me."

Mama banged around in the cupboard again. "Goodness, I was sure I'd put my Pyrex measuring cup on this shelf."

"Uh . . . I'll guess you'll have to use the tin measuring cup. Mimi and I used it last night to make fudge, and it works fine."

"It doesn't have a pouring spout," complained Mama, crashing the pans and bowls around a few times more. "I like a measuring cup with a spout."

So there was nothing to do but tell Mom the whole story. About how Mimi and I had wanted to find out if the Spikeses were really midgets. About how we'd decided to play detective and go over to Mrs. Overfield's to borrow vinegar. About how we'd accidentally left Mom's Pyrex measuring cup over there on account of we'd suddenly had to beat it for the door.

She picked up the tin measuring cup, frowned at it, and set it down again. "Well, go get my measuring cup back. I want to make some muffins."

"Oh, Mom, that tin cup is really great. You can level things off at the top with it. You can't do that when a measuring cup has a spout."

"Kimberly," Mom said, using the name she calls me only when she means business, "I want my Pyrex cup back. Go get it."

"Do I have to?"

"Yes." Mama put her hands on my back and

102

edged me toward the door. Then her tone changed. "Don't think of it as an order from your chemically imbalanced mother. Think of it as an opportunity to play detective again."

Funny. Very funny.

I could think of a hundred reasons why I didn't want to go back to Mrs. Overfield's, beginning with the color of my legs. With all the red welts from the tams junipers and the blue bruises from Bubba Joe's feet, my shins looked like a pair of American flags. I stood on our front porch rubbing them.

"Go on, Kim," Mama commanded. "And keep your eyes open over there. Maybe you'll learn something important."

Cripes.

"Right now," Mama insisted.

I sighed, knowing how determined Mama could get and how I might as well get things over with. I threw my shoulders back and started off, hoping that Calvin would be the one to open the door. Of all those freckled lunatics next door, he seemed to be the least dangerous one.

As if he'd read my thoughts, Calvin exploded out of Mrs. Overfield's front door right that very minute, together with all three cats. He was carrying Thomas Jefferson, but Dolley Madison and

Harry Truman were walking by themselves. Dolley and Harry had brand new kitty-cat collars around their necks tied to long chains.

I rushed over to meet him. "Calvin, I left my mother's glass measuring cup over here last night. Will you go get it for me?"

"Nope."

I guess I should have expected some sort of answer like that, but it startled me, anyway. "Uh—please. My mother really needs it."

"Get it yourself," he suggested.

You could be almost sure he didn't mean that as an invitation, but maybe he did. Still, I sure didn't want to bump into any other Spikeses inside the door. "Is—is anyone else home?" I said.

"No. DeVeda took Earl and Bubba Joe out. I couldn't go because I have to take my cats for a walk. I'm teaching Thomas Jefferson to heel." And with that he set the cat down.

"Do you know where Mama's cup is?" I asked.

"Yep."

A pause.

"*Where?*" I demanded. Sometimes those Spikeses could be so rude and bratty you'd like to smack them.

"On the coffee table."

"Thanks," I said.

He turned his back to me and walked off without so much as a good-bye. The amazing thing was that Dolley Madison and Harry Truman, who never did anything for Mrs. Overfield but eat or sleep or scratch her furniture with their sharp claws, actually walked along with him on their leashes. And Thomas Jefferson followed properly behind, as smart as any dog you'll ever see on graduation day at obedience school.

I noticed something else, too. Every time before when I'd seen the Spikeses, they were either going barefoot or wearing thongs. Today Calvin was sporting a pair of classy blue-and-white Reebok hightops that were about six sizes too big for him and exactly like a pair I'd seen Mrs. Overfield wearing one Sunday.

But I didn't have time to worry about other people's shoes. I had to sneak in and out of Mrs. Overfield's house for Mama's measuring cup before those three other Spikeses got home.

I opened the door and walked in, planning to go straight to the coffee table, but something terrible caught my eye. In place of the Japanese print that had been hanging in the living room was one of those five bigger-than-life-size photographs of her ex-husbands that always stared out at you from over the bed in Mrs. Overfield's room. What had happened to the Japanese print? Had one of the Spikeses been able to open the safe behind it?

And how many other things were missing?

I wanted to look around and see but was afraid Bone Crusher Earl and Granite Toes Bubba Joe might walk in and catch me in the act. So I rushed to the coffee table instead.

Oh, yuck!

Inside Mama's Pyrex measuring cup was an oozy brown mass of cut-up worms.

Dizzy. I felt dizzy.

I looked around for some box or bag to dump them in, but I couldn't see a thing except Mrs. Overfield's crystal candy dish, which had the bad luck to be sitting right next to Mama's Pyrex cup on the coffee table.

I realize it was an awful, terrible thing to do, but sometimes you just don't think clearly in an emergency. I turned Mama's measuring cup upside down over the candy dish and shook it. A few of those pieces of cut-up worm fell out, but most of them stuck together like mush, so I had to reach in with my fingers to scrape out the rest.

Ooooh!

Holding my clean hand over my mouth, I raced all the way home, handed the cup to

Mama, and barked, "Boil this for half an hour before you use it."

Then I ran into the bathroom and shut the door so I could throw up.

13

Later, after I'd explained to Mom why she'd had to boil the measuring cup and after we'd eaten practically a whole batch of oat bran muffins, I found her in her study. She was sitting at her desk, chomping as if she had a whole New York steak in her mouth, not just five little sticks of Black Jack gum. Her Life Experience notebook was on the desk in front of her, and she was making squiggly red marks in the margins.

I sat down quietly in the empty chair so I wouldn't disturb her. But she knew I was there.

"I used to think that constructing a plot for a

novel was the hardest job in the world," she sighed, "but that's apple pie compared to trying to figure out what's going on next door. Or getting anyone else to believe the part I have figured out."

"Didn't Creative Search work?" I asked.

"Not exactly. The only thing I can think of is to go back to the police station again. But I sure don't want to go back and face either of those two desk sergeants we've met so far."

"Maybe they'll believe us this time."

Mama opened a new pack of Black Jack. "Maybe glaciers aren't cold. Maybe California won't ever have another earthquake. Maybe I'll make fifty thousand dollars this year. Maybe—"

"They've got to believe us this time," I argued. "They've just got to."

Mom unwrapped a stick of gum and stared at it. "Yeah, but we need a new angle. Something they'll listen to."

"They'd listen if you told them the Spikeses are dealing in drugs. You could tell them that we've seen suspicious people coming over all the time to buy drugs."

"Kim!" Mama exclaimed. "That's an out-and-out lie."

"Not exactly. I saw a suspicious-looking man

ringing their doorbell yesterday."

"You mean the same man who rang our doorbell asking if he could wash our windows?"

"Yes," I admitted, "but maybe he just said that at our house because he rang our bell by mistake. He might have been looking for the Spikeses to buy drugs from them."

"We're not going to tell the police any lies. They really won't believe us if we start telling deliberate lies."

"Well, how about if we told them that the Spikes kids said they're Mrs. Overfield's relatives from Australia? But we're afraid they probably stowed away on some airplane because they arrived in Salt Lake halfway across the world without any grown-ups with them or anyone in town here to meet them."

"You know something? That idea is so preposterous it might actually be true. Sometimes the most preposterous idea turns out to be the right one. But we'd certainly need more proof than we have already before we try to convince those callous desk sergeants." Mama folded the stick of gum into fourths and put in her mouth. "Policemen always want some kind of evidence."

Inside my skull I felt an idea burst like a giant kernel of popcorn. "Evidence? How about the testimony of the social worker assigned to the case?"

Mama knitted her eyebrows. You could tell she was nervous about any idea involving Ms. Freymuller.

"Let's tell the police that the Spikeses are midgets," I said.

"Oh tish! Just because that poor little Ms. Freymuller believes that all children are sweet and adorable doesn't mean that any hard-boiled policemen are going to be taken in by that midget story."

"Look at it this way. The police are more likely to help us if they think we're dealing with adult criminals and not a bunch of juvenile delinquents. And besides, there's always a chance that Ms. Freymuller might have been right. You said yourself that the most preposterous story might be the true one."

Mama sat, silent, chewing on those possibilities as hard as she was chewing on her gum. While she was doing that, I told her about the other things I'd seen today: Calvin wearing the familiar-looking pair of Reebok hightops and the photograph of one of Mrs. Overfield's ex-husbands hanging in her living room in the place of her framed Japanese print.

That did it. Mom took the big wad of gum out of her mouth, wrapped it in paper, and tossed it into the wastebasket. "Well, just because up to now the police haven't taken Mrs. Overfield's problems seriously doesn't mean that I'm going to die without trying to convince them." She stood up, a new look of determination on her face. Mama tucked the Life Experience notebook under her arm. "Let's go."

When we got to the garage, I could hardly squeeze into my side of the Celebrity. The way DeVeda had parked the Thunderbird used up more than her half of the space, and it hardly seemed fair, even if she did have to avoid hitting all the bags of garbage the Spikeses had lined up against the wall.

"How could four little kids make so much garbage?" I complained.

"Maybe those bags are where Bubba Joe keeps his supply of cut-up worms," Mom suggested.

Shuddering, I got into the car and sat at Mom's side the whole way to town without speaking another word.

Like Mama, I'd been hoping that a new desk sergeant would be on duty—someone who respected women and children and took their complaints seriously. But it was just our luck to

112

find the first officer back at the desk, the one who looked like a Yellowstone Park buffalo.

The worst of it was, he even remembered Mama and me.

"Well, did you find the Chinese silk purse with your neighbor's keys in it?" he asked.

"No," Mom said, "but I'm sure I know who did."

"I'm sure you do," he said.

Mom let the sarcasm pass. "Yes, a family of—uh—midgets." Even though Mama didn't believe what she was saying, she's a really good actress sometimes, especially when important things like all Mrs. Overfield's collections and our own family honor are on the line.

"Midgets? I thought you said it was a giant who stole the purse. Someone who looks like Larry Bird." He sucked in his cheeks, trying not to grin.

You have to admire the way Mama can pretend not to notice certain things. She just went right on explaining, as polite as could be. "A tall man *stole* the purse, all right. But a family of midgets—or maybe they're children—must have found the keys, because they've moved themselves into Mrs. Overfield's house and have taken over everything she owns."

This time the desk sergeant had to turn his entire head so we wouldn't see his face. About five years passed before he got control of himself and looked back at Mama again. "I take it you've come to file a complaint against the—the midgets?"

"Yes. As I said, they could be children, though. Anyway, I do know their name is Spikes—unless that's an alias, of course."

"Alias? Spikes?" he sputtered. "Hey, Al, come listen to this with me, will you? I—I—I—" He was doubled over, holding his stomach. "I want to make sure we get it right."

Al came right over to help. So did another man in uniform and two ladies. The committee of them punched a few words into the computer and decided there was no family of midgets—or children, either—named Spikes who were wanted for any crimes in any of the United States. But of course that was just a preliminary check and nothing definite. Maybe we'd like to come back after we'd learned the criminals' real name, not just their alias.

As we walked out the door, we heard a chorus of laughter, louder than the Mormon Tabernacle Choir.

I felt awful, even worse than when we'd been

standing there with the desk sergeant bent over like a paper clip, laughing his insides out. "Mom, I'm sorry I made you go back and talk to the police again."

"You didn't make me. And sooner or later I would have thought of using that midget routine myself. Well, we might as well put this outing to some use. Want to go to the library and check out some books?"

I nodded. Real life is too confusing. I wanted something that makes sense, like stories.

14

Dad came home from Park City on Saturday, but he wasn't much help.

"You're overdramatizing again, Janice," he said, after Mom and I had listed all the events of the past two weeks. "I'm sure there's a perfectly simple explanation for what's going on next door, and you should stop worrying about problems that don't exist. You need to get away for a while and stop thinking about Mrs. Overfield's house. Now that you have no reason to stay home and tend the cats, why don't you and Kim come to San Francisco with me?"

"You know we can't afford that."

Dad sighed. "Well, at least you can go to Park City. The hotel gave me a free pass for a Saturday-night stay and the Sunday-morning brunch. The two of you can go up there tonight after you've taken me to the airport."

Mom nodded and accepted the pass he offered as if she were agreeing with him, which she wasn't. She and I both knew what we'd seen with our own eyes and heard with our own ears.

But the whole thing was turning out to be a very lonely Life Experience. No one in our family believed us, and we'd even run out of government agencies we could call on for help, except maybe the fire department. But Mama didn't think it was a very good idea to put in a false alarm so the firemen would come roaring out to Mrs. Overfield's house with all their ladders and hoses and hatchets.

So the two of us spent the week by ourselves, reading the books we'd checked out of the library and peeking out the window (for any new crimes that crazy pack of hyenas might be committing). About all we saw, though, was DeVeda polishing Mrs. Overfield's car one afternoon and Calvin going outside very early each morning to walk Dolley Madison and Harry Truman and

Thomas Jefferson.

On Friday Mama was so frustrated that she actually baked one of her famous German chocolate cakes and took it over to the Spikeses in hopes that they might invite her into Mrs. Overfield's house so she could inspect it for any missing items. But Earl answered the bell, grabbed the cake out of her hands, and slammed the door in her face without even saying thank you.

All in all it was a pretty dull week and not very useful, so Mom decided that maybe Dad was right and we needed to get away. On Saturday the two of us packed our swimming suits and our sunscreen and a couple of thousand crossword puzzles and headed for Park City.

After we'd lain in the sun all day Saturday and watched movies until two A.M. and stuffed ourselves sick on the croissants at Sunday brunch, it was time to check out, so we did. I guess we both dreaded going home, because instead of heading to the car we decided to window-shop at all the fancy tourist boutiques along Park City's Main Street.

A few stores were open, but not many, because it was a Sunday in July and not exactly the height of the ski season. We walked slowly, admiring all the $500 handknit sweaters in the windows and wondering what kind of people could afford them. Then, in the window of an antique store, I saw something that gave me cold chills, right there in the ninety-eight-degree sunshine.

"*Mama!*" I shrieked.

"For goodness sake, Kim, you scared me to death."

I was shivering so hard the finger I was pointing with shook. "*There's Mrs. Overfield's jade Buddha, the one she keeps in her bathroom!*"

"Lower your voice, dear," said Mom without turning her head. "Of course that isn't Mrs. Overfield's. Look at this sweet little cradle over here. If I thought your sister might ever have a baby, I'd love to buy it for her."

"Look at the Buddha, Mama!"

"Goodness, Kim, stop yelling. People are staring at us."

"But it's Mrs. Overfield's Buddha! Those Spikeses stole it and gave it to this antiques store to sell it to some tourist!"

"Oh tish. No one would be stupid enough to steal a valuable antique and then turn right around and sell it in broad daylight, not fifty miles away."

"The Spikeses might be that stupid," I suggested.

I guess Mama thought that possibility was worth considering, because she stopped looking at the baby cradle and walked over to where I was standing. "Oh my goodness! My goodness! That does look exactly like Mrs. Overfield's Buddha!"

The store was closed, of course, it being an off-season Sunday and all, and not a big day for antiques. And Mama and I had already checked out of our hotel.

So we decided to drive home to sleep, and then come back first thing Monday morning to talk to the store owner.

But of course we didn't know that something would happen the next day to ruin our plans.

15

Just as Mama picked up her purse and we started toward the back door to drive to Park City on Monday morning, the front doorbell rang. Mama and I both sprang to answer.

All the Spikeses were there, their feet lined up on our top step like a picture from a brand-new sportswear catalog: Nike, Reebok, British Knights, L. A. Gear. Well! As if it hadn't been bad enough to see Mrs. Overfield's Chinese jade Buddha for sale in an antique store in Park City. Now we had to find her world-class hightops on all those no-class Spikes feet. But I didn't have a chance to say anything because all the Spikeses started talking at once.

"Have you seen our cat?"

"Where's our cat?"

"What did you do with our cat?"

"We want Thomas Jefferson!"

Mama and I exchanged looks of horror. Of all her possessions, Mrs. Overfield loved Thomas Jefferson the most, and we knew she'd be more upset by his disappearance than by the unauthorized use of her personal hightops or any of the other million terrible things that had happened to her car and her house and her collections up to now.

"We haven't seen Thomas Jefferson," Mama said.

"You said you wanted to take care of the cats," I added. "We've never seen them except when Calvin takes them outside for walks."

"You're lying." Earl elbowed his way past Mama and me and into our hall. The others followed behind, and once inside, the four of them scattered through our house like a plague of locusts, opening doors, moving furniture, peeking into drawers and cupboards.

"Here, Thomas Jefferson."

"Here, kitty, kitty, kitty."

"Come on, Tom, come on."

"Here, Tom. Let's go home and get some nice cat food."

But Thomas Jefferson didn't appear, and after about five thousand years the Spikeses realized we weren't hiding him.

"What do we do now?" wailed Calvin.

"Shut up and let me think," said DeVeda.

"How long has he been missing?" Mom asked.

"I didn't notice until yesterday morning—Sunday," Calvin said. "Bubba Joe left the door open Saturday night, and—"

"It wasn't my fault," said Bubba Joe. "You always say everything's my fault."

Calvin held firm. "Bubba Joe left the door open all night, and someone snuck in and stole Thomas Jefferson."

"You can't be sure anyone did that," Mama argued. "Maybe the cat just walked away."

"He wouldn't do no such thing. He wouldn't never leave me!" said Calvin.

"He might if he smelled a girl cat outside," I said.

"He loves me more than any old girl cat," said Calvin.

"He loves me more than he loves you," said Bubba Joe.

"We can't waste time arguing," Mama said. "We've got to look for him. Let's divide up into teams and scout the neighborhood. DeVeda and Earl, you two can be on one team. Kim can go with Calvin. And Bubba Joe can go with me."

I couldn't imagine why Mama volunteered to go with Bubba Joe unless I'd never bothered to tell her why my legs had turned purple, but I didn't see any reason to mention it now.

Calvin and I started up Sigsbee Avenue, looking under bushes and up trees and knocking on people's doors. With every headshake or "No, I haven't seen a Siamese cat," I got more and more discouraged about ever returning Mrs. Overfield's favorite possession to her. I was almost sure that Thomas Jefferson had finally taken all he was willing to from those lunatic Spikeses and had run away from our neighborhood and Salt Lake City and possibly the whole state of Utah.

Then, when I was just about to tell Calvin that I didn't think there was any point in looking further and we might as well go home, something happened. I looked at Calvin's face and saw the pain on it and realized he loved Thomas Jefferson every bit as much as Mrs. Overfield did, possibly even more.

"Here, kitty," I called. "Here, kitty, kitty, kitty."

"Thomas Jefferson!" shouted Calvin.

At the sound of Calvin's voice a cat crawled out from under the snowball bush growing on the grass island where Sigsbee Avenue intersects with Perry Avenue and Wolcott Street. From the distance I couldn't be absolutely positive it was a Siamese, but I thought it was.

As soon as the cat stepped off the curb and into the street, Calvin saw it too and started running toward it. *"Thomas Jefferson! Thomas Jefferson!"*

Just then a red Mercury came barreling down the hill and careened around the island on two wheels, the teenage girls inside it shrieking like a party of witches. The car hardly even slowed down, and after it passed the island and raced down Perry Avenue, we could see a light-brown cat lying in the street.

We both ran toward the animal as fast as we could. "Thomas Jefferson!" Calvin howled.

It wasn't a pretty sight—lots of blood and matted fur.

You might have expected Calvin to charge after the car, shaking his fist and cursing, but he didn't. Instead, he took off his very own T-shirt and placed it over Thomas Jefferson to keep the cat warm.

I guess the noise of the car and Calvin's yelling worried the other Spikeses and Mama, because pretty soon all of them came running. By then Calvin was huddled over the cat, whispering, "Don't die. Please don't die."

"Oh, Tom!" wailed Bubba Joe. "It's him!"

DeVeda dropped to her knees beside Calvin. "Oh, don't die, Thomas Jefferson. I promise I'll do anything in this world if you won't die."

"Me, too," echoed Earl. "I'll do anything you want. Please don't die."

They were all crying. Those four mean, selfish, utterly awful Spikeses were crying as if they actually cared about something besides themselves. It made you wonder if they might not even be a little bit human, after all.

"Maybe we should take him to a vet," I suggested.

But I was just trying to cheer everyone up. Deep in my heart I knew it was too late for a vet to do any good.

16

After Earl wrapped Thomas Jefferson in his and Calvin's and Bubba Joe's shirts to carry the cat to Mrs. Overfield's house, Mama and I went home to our own bedrooms for a good cry. Later, I overheard Mom telephoning around town to find out how much a new Siamese cat would cost. I guess she figured that she was partly responsible for Thomas Jefferson's death and that Mrs. Overfield might not take the loss so hard— we all might not take the loss so hard—if we had another Siamese cat to love.

Mama was on the phone when the front doorbell rang, so I went to the door to see who was there. Actually, no one was there—there was just a piece of paper lying on the porch, as if someone had left a Valentine and run. I picked up the note to read it:

Mrs. Sanders and Kim.
Your invited to the funral of T. Jefferson today at 4 o'clock. Bring flours.

"Isn't that sweet?" Mom wiped a new tear away when I showed her the invitation. "Of course you can cut some gladiola blossoms if you want to." Then she showed me which vase to use and I went out in back with a pair of scissors.

Across the tams junipers in Mrs. Overfield's half of the backyard, all four Spikeses were digging a deep hole, and for once they didn't seem to be hitting each other or yelling or even talking. I decided they were trying to show their respect for Thomas Jefferson by keeping quiet, so I didn't yell "Hi" or anything across the junipers.

I also didn't bother to tell them that I was pretty sure that what they were doing was against the law. I don't think you're allowed to bury dead animals in your backyard—at least not in our neighborhood—but I've never been able to figure out why not. Anyhow, up to this point the Salt Lake City Police Department hadn't seemed very interested in any laws that were being broken at Mrs. Overfield's house, and I didn't suppose anyone was likely to come nosying around now.

I made a beautiful arrangement of gladiola blooms—all shades of red and pink and peach and yellow—and then I took a shower and put on my best pair of jeans and a clean blouse. Mom got dressed up, too, in her dark-blue summer skirt, and we walked next door without talking.

I suppose the Spikeses had seen funerals in a few movies or something, because they more or less knew what to do. They'd put folding chairs out in back for people to sit on, and Thomas Jefferson was lying in a cardboard box so we could all pass by him for a final viewing.

DeVeda put my bouquet of gladiola blooms right next to the box, and then she led us all in the chorus of a song from *Cats*. (She was the only one who knew the words.) After the music was over, DeVeda called on Calvin to speak "because he was the person who knew Thomas Jefferson best."

I half expected Bubba Joe to pop out of his seat right that minute and go kick DeVeda in the shins, but he didn't. He just sat quietly with his arms folded, which was something you didn't see happen every day.

Calvin stood up and walked to the front, his face red and puffy from crying. "Dearly beloved, one of our choicest brethren has passed to the Great Beyond for Cats—"

Meow!

Calvin's eyebrows shot up like a pair of express elevators. Of course people tell stories all the time about how cats have nine lives, but just the same, it was pretty scary to think that a cat you knew for an absolute fact was dead might be *meow*ing right in the middle of his own funeral.

Calvin rushed over to the cardboard box to see if the noise was coming from there. It wasn't.

"I think it was Harry Truman or Dolley Madison," he said. "I think they must be crying because they weren't invited to the funeral. I'll go get them."

"I'll go with you," said DeVeda.

So the funeral was delayed for a few minutes while the two other cats were brought to the backyard, wearing their kitty-cat collars and leashes. Calvin tied the leashes to the porch railing, and both cats curled up and fell asleep.

"As I was saying," Calvin went on, "one of our beloved brethren has been called home—"

Meow!

You could be sure that Dolley Madison and Harry Truman were too sound asleep to make that noise. And Thomas Jefferson was out cold in the cardboard box. So who was doing that *meowing?*

Just then something tan jumped from the garage roof and landed on Calvin's shoulder. Whatever it was knocked Calvin to the ground, so we all ran over to help.

"Thomas Jefferson!" cried Calvin.

"Thomas Jefferson!" cried DeVeda.

"Thomas Jefferson!" cried Earl.

"Who the heck is dead around here?" complained Bubba Joe.

The Spikeses had to find out, of course, so they carried the live cat over to the dead one to compare the two.

During the confusion I sidled up to Mom and whispered in her ear.

"That cat is a new one you just bought, isn't it? I heard you making phone calls to buy one."

"Of course not," said Mama. "You know I haven't been out of the house all day. Besides, all

131

those cat owners wanted too much money. I couldn't afford a purebred Siamese."

So Mom and I joined the others, and all of us took turns examining the two cats. When we were through, we voted one hundred percent that the live cat was the real Thomas Jefferson. For one thing, he did what he was told when Calvin ordered him to heel. For another, he had a little nick in his left ear that Dolley Madison had put there years ago.

Then we all hugged each other and cried a little.

"Isn't it wonderful?" Calvin exclaimed. "Thomas Jefferson didn't die, after all."

"It's a miracle," DeVeda agreed.

No one knew who the dead cat was, or who he might belong to, but we hated to let a good funeral go to waste, so we buried him.

We all decided it was the best funeral we'd ever been to. And everyone went home happy.

17

When Mama and I got to Park City the next day, we had to leave the car about a thousand miles away and take a shuttle bus to Main Street.

"I forgot that the Summer Arts Festival was going on this week," Mama said. "There are always so many people at the festival that someone is bound to see Mrs. Overfield's Buddha and want to buy it. I sure hope it isn't already gone."

"It won't be," I said. "Nobody but Mrs. Overfield would be crazy enough to want a jade Buddha, even in her bathroom."

But when we got to Main Street and I saw

exactly two million pedestrians walking up and down the narrow road, I began to worry a little, too. They were all rich tourists from California. You could tell that they were rich because the men wore heavy gold chains around their necks and diamond rings on their pinkie fingers, and the women wore clothes with labels that said GIVENCHY and GUCCI and CALVIN KLEIN. And you knew they were from California because that's where all the rich people who come to Park City actually live. Aside from Mrs. Overfield, I figured, rich tourists from California were the only non-Buddhists in the world who might spend perfectly good money on a little green statue.

Main Street was lined with booths on both sides. Artists and craftspeople were selling their wares, everything you can imagine: porcelain jewelry, bamboo furniture, oil-on-velvet paintings, watercolor landscapes, charcoal caricatures, feathered hats, tie-dyed T-shirts. Some of it was okay, but lots of the stuff seemed pretty junky, and you couldn't have paid me to carry it home.

The street was so crowded, we walked a block too far before we realized we'd passed the antique store that we'd come to see. We turned around and walked back to look in the store window.

"Oh, Mama! The jade Buddha is gone!"

"Goodness!" Mom wailed. "I was afraid of that!"

"What do we do now?"

"We go inside the store and talk to those people, of course. I didn't drive all the way from Salt Lake just to look through a piece of glass."

But the saleslady was no help. She couldn't remember ever seeing a jade Buddha in the store. And the owner had just left to go to Mexico City on a buying trip. Mama wrote down his name and phone number and the approximate date he'd be home in her Life Experience notebook. But that was about all we could do right that moment in Park City except look at all the crafts booths and buy some hamburgers and nachos from a sidewalk vendor and have our pictures drawn by one of the caricaturists and stop for a dozen Mrs. Fields' cookies on our way to the shuttle bus. Besides having "the greatest snow on earth," Park City is famous for being the home of Mrs. Fields' cookies, so I figure it's a matter of principle to buy some every time we go there.

Driving home, we planned the next thing we

should do—find some excuse to visit Mrs. Over-field's bathroom and see if her jade Buddha was actually missing. Maybe the one we'd seen in the antique store window wasn't really hers. And maybe—since we'd more or less become friends at "Thomas Jefferson's" funeral—the Spikeses would let us in their house now.

When we reached Salt Lake it was time for dinner, but Mom and I weren't hungry after all the junk food we'd been eating, so we went straight to Mrs. Overfield's house and rang the doorbell.

You could have knocked me over with a puff of smoke when Mrs. Overfield herself answered the door.

"Goodness!" Mama cried. "How did you get here?"

"In my car, of course," Mrs. Overfield said. "I was sorry you didn't feel well enough to come to the airport. Are you better now?"

"Better?" said Mom. "I'm not sick. I'm perfectly fine."

"I'm so glad," Mrs. Overfield gushed. "Anyway, I got the message you left for me on the white paging telephone—"

Mama looked stunned. "I didn't leave you a message."

But Mrs. Overfield went right on talking. "So I picked up my Chinese silk purse with my keys and the note you left about the location of the car at the Delta message desk."

I turned to Mama. "Do you think the Spikeses could have—?"

Mom shrugged. "They must have. Who else could it be?"

"Come into the living room and sit down," Mrs. Overfield interrupted, leading us there. "I don't know how I can ever thank you for all you did for me."

When we reached the living room, I pointed to the wall. "Look! The Japanese print!"

"It's there!" Mama cried. "Isn't that wonderful!"

"Of course it's there," said Mrs. Overfield. "That's where I always keep it. Oh, sit down, please."

I plopped down on the sofa, but on the coffee table I noticed something that made my stomach turn a double gainer. Mrs. Overfield—or someone—had just ruined a perfectly good supply of chocolate-covered caramels by putting them in Bubba Joe's yucky cut-up-worm dish. I edged away from the dish.

"I don't know how I'll ever thank you for taking such good care of things," Mrs. Overfield burbled. "I swear my house has never been this clean."

"Oh, I didn't clean it," Mom said. "It must have been the children."

"Children? What children?" asked Mrs. Overfield.

"Earl and DeVeda and Calvin and Bubba Joe," I offered. "Do you have any nieces and nephews named Earl and DeVeda and Calvin and Bubba Joe?"

Mrs. Overfield squinched up her eyes to think. "My nephew Kenneth has a boy named Melvin. Or is it Martin?"

"Do you have any relatives named Spikes?" Mama asked.

"No," said Mrs. Overfield.

"They said you were their aunt," I offered.

"Not if their name is Spikes. I'm sure I'd remember anyone named Spikes." Mrs. Overfield swept her arm around in the air. "Oh! I can't get over what a wonderful job you did for me. My Venus's-flytraps have never looked so healthy and the cats have improved their manners remarkably. Why, Thomas Jefferson even comes now when I call him! Imagine!"

"Uh—I don't suppose you've noticed if anything might be missing—your diamonds or anything?" Mama said.

"Of course not. What would be missing?"

"Did you look in your safe?"

"As a matter of fact I did, if you really want to know. I bought a new diamond ring in New York and decided to put it away in my safe. Everything else was in there, just as I left it."

"May I please use your bathroom?" I asked.

"Of course, dear," Mrs. Overfield said.

As I walked down the hall, I was hoping so hard that the jade Buddha would be on the bathroom vanity where it belonged that I guess my knees shook a little. But I wasn't hoping it for my sake or Mama's or even Mrs. Overfield's. I was hoping for the Spikeses' sakes that they'd realized the promises they made when they thought Thomas Jefferson was dying were important, and they'd decided to keep them.

Sure enough, the jade Buddha was in the bathroom, and in my heart I guess I said a little prayer of thanks.

I know people don't change overnight. But maybe the Spikeses still had time to do a little changing in their lives. Maybe Earl would grow up to be a bodyguard for an important person, like the president. Maybe DeVeda would grow

139

up to be the head of a worthwhile group, like the National Organization for Women. Maybe Calvin would grow up to be an animal trainer at, say, the San Diego Zoo. Maybe Bubba Joe would grow up to be a placekicker for the San Francisco 49ers.

I must have been smiling as I walked back into the living room and gave Mama the thumbs-up sign to let her know that Mrs. Overfield's jade Buddha was safe.

"Oh, stop telling me that ridiculous story about children living in my house while I was away," Mrs. Overfield was saying. "I know you're just being modest about taking such good care of things. Now what can I get you to drink? Lemonade? Iced tea? Diet Coke?"

Mama said she didn't have time for a drink right now. She wanted to go straight home and write down some very important facts in her Life Experience notebook before she forgot them, because she might decide to write a very unusual children's novel someday.

"Well, you can at least take time for a caramel," Mrs. Overfield insisted, passing the cut-up-worm dish to Mama.

Mom took a caramel from the dish and actually ate it.

"I know you'd like some candy, too, wouldn't you, Kim?"

How could I refuse an invitation like that?

I took a piece of candy and bit into it. It didn't taste bad at all. In fact, it really tasted great.

"Have another," said Mrs. Overfield.

"Thank you," I said. "I don't mind if I do."

18

The next week Darci and Jannalee and Brynne all came home from their vacations, so life settled pretty much back to normal. Every day some or all of us would go to one of the downtown malls to window-shop for our school clothes. Not that any of us had any money to spend.

Unlike Mimi's parents, ours always waited until the last possible moment before school started to hand over any cash. But it was important to decide what we wanted in advance and to know where all the bargains were, so we had to go shopping every day. Mom teased that we just went to the mall to cruise for boys, but that's only because someone who hasn't attended junior high for nearly a thousand years doesn't understand how important it is to wear exactly the right clothes to Bryant Junior High School, especially the first week of school.

One Friday in late August, Jannalee and Brynne had gone to a family reunion at Bear Lake, so Darci and I went shopping together. After we'd tried on ten or twelve blouses each and maybe a dozen pairs of shoes, we were tired and hungry and needed some lunch, so we went to the snack bar in the ZCMI basement for some of their terrific homemade bread with melted cheese. Rob Farrell's older brother is a busboy, so sometimes Rob hangs out in the snack bar. I don't like him especially, but Darci thinks Rob is *kee-yute*. Anyway, it didn't matter right then because Rob wasn't there.

Everyone else was there, though, if you count secretaries on their lunch hours and old ladies with shopping bags and dirty-faced kids whining to go home. Every single seat was taken at every single table, so Darci and I decided that she'd go order the food while I watched the tables to pounce on the first two seats that someone vacated.

That's how I happened to overhear an important conversation. I didn't plan to eavesdrop or anything. I just happened to be standing right behind a big plant where anyone couldn't help hearing what I did because a lady who was sitting at a nearby table was talking so loudly to her two kids.

"Do you realize the only thing you've told me about summer camp is those three cats you trained?"

I pricked my ears up at that, all right. Nobody in the whole world ever tried to train cats except that crazy Calvin Spikes. Holding my breath, I peeked between some leaves to get a better look at the people who were talking.

Sure enough, one of the kids sitting at that table was Calvin. You didn't have to be a rocket scientist to figure that out, even from the back, or to know that the girl at the table was DeVeda. Anyone would have recognized their frizzy red hair.

"Well?" the woman said. She was hunched over the table, coaxing for details about the kids' lives, just like any mother would.

I don't suppose it had ever occurred to me

144

before that the Spikeses might have a mother, not a normal mother anyway. But here this woman was, with a Ralph Lauren polo shirt and a Gucci shoulder bag and two spots of pink under her huge brown eyes, looking almost like a younger version of my own mother and talking exactly like her.

"It was hot," Calvin said.

"It was weird," said DeVeda.

"But what did you *do*? When your father and I spent over five thousand dollars to send all of you to that camp, we expected you to *do* something."

"They make you do plenty at that awful camp. They make you do something weird every single minute," DeVeda said. "That's why I didn't want to go back this year. And why I won't ever go back there again."

"There was lots of spiders and beetles," Calvin explained. "It was my job to collect all the spiders and beetles I could find and save them. And Bubba Joe's job was to find all the worms so he could cut them up into little bitsy pieces and put them in a candy dish."

"*What?*" said Mrs. Spikes.

"I told you it was a weird place," DeVeda chirped.

Mrs. Spikes rolled her eyes at the ceiling. "Calvin, did DeVeda tell you to say that? About collecting spiders and beetles? And cutting up worms?"

"Uh-uh. That's what me and Bubba Joe had to do. Cross my heart and hope to wrestle a snake. When I wasn't training Thomas Jefferson and Dolley Madison and Harry Truman, I didn't do nothing but collect bugs. And Bubba Joe spent every single minute cutting up worms."

"Well!" Mrs. Spikes brushed her hair back from her forehead. She looked wilted. "We'll talk about that when we get home. I want to go buy a raspberry pie for tonight's dinner. I'll be back in a few minutes." And she stood up.

As soon as she was out of earshot, Calvin leaned toward his sister. "I did good, didn't I, telling her about the spiders and beetles and cut-up worms?"

"I don't know. She's getting suspicious. What if she should telephone Mr. Halstead and complain?"

"You said she can't telephone Mr. Halstead," Calvin said. "You said there isn't no telephone at that camp."

"No, but she could write him a letter. And then Mr. Halstead could go to that store in town

146

and telephone her. Don't tell her one more thing about what we did this summer except I say so. You and Bubba Joe have never been to that camp, so you're like as not to say dumb things that will give us away. And we'll be in big trouble if she ever decides to write to Mr. Halstead."

From the corner of my eye I saw a couple of teenagers vacating a table on the other side of the room, but there was no way I'd go sit down so far away and miss the rest of this conversation. Instead, I crouched lower behind the plant that kept me pretty well hidden from the Spikeses' table.

"I don't say no dumb things," Calvin argued. "Bubba Joe's the dummy. He's the one who blabbed about the letter from Mr. Halstead. Lucky thing no one never believes what that stupid kid says."

"You mean it was lucky I was home that day when the letter came. If Mom had seen that refund check Mr. Halstead sent 'cause we never showed up at camp, we'd all be grounded for the rest of our born lives."

"What are you going to do with that check?"

DeVeda started breaking her cheese bread into little pieces. "Cash it."

"You wouldn't dare try," Calvin said.

"Someone's got to. If no one cashes a check for five thousand two hundred and twenty-four dollars, Mr. Halstead will sure as heck wonder how come. And then he'll telephone Mom. And then she'll find out about the letter we wrote him to cancel our reservations."

"Yeah," Calvin agreed.

"So it's up to the only person in this family with brains bigger than a pea to figure out how to do it."

"Just 'cause you're always bragging you have an IQ of a hundred and forty-six doesn't mean you can cash no check without no ID."

"Says you."

"How?" Calvin demanded. "Just how you think you're going to do it?"

"Listen, Calvin, I've told you a million times. You can do anything in this world if you really want to." DeVeda's tone suddenly changed. "Especially if you know the right people."

"Just what right people do you think you know?"

"Somebody."

"Joe Turley! I bet you mean Joe Turley."

"Mmm. Maybe," DeVeda admitted.

"Joe Turley doesn't have no five thousand two

148

hundred and twenty-four dollars. His daddy only pays him six fifty an hour to work in that stupid antique store in Park City."

"Maybe Joe doesn't have the money himself, but everyone in Park City knows his dad is an important businessman. And they know Joe is his kid. I'll get Joe to drive me to a bank in Park City and help me get the check cashed. He believes anything I tell him."

"That's for sure. That dummy even believed your stupid story about our poor grandmother who had cancer and how we had to sell all her vases and statues to pay for her drug treatments."

DeVeda giggled. "I'll never forget his face the first night we met him. Remember how he almost cried real tears into his frozen yogurt when I told him about our grandmama?"

"Poor Joe! First he drove all Mrs. Overfield's stuff to Park City in his truck to try to sell it for us in his daddy's store up there. And then he drove it all back again when you told him someone else had offered to pay cash right away."

"So now"—DeVeda waved her hand in the air—"so now I'll just tell him Mr. Halstead is the guy who bought the stuff. But no one will cash the check Mr. Halstead mailed us because our grandmother's sick in the hospital and I can't find her ID."

"Well—it might work. Joe Turley is so dumb he can't whistle and tie his shoes at the same time."

"Sure it will work. Trust me. Did I get Mrs. Overfield's house cleaned and back in shape before she got home when all you guys said I couldn't? Well, I'll get that check cashed, too. And I'll hide the money where no one can find it, so if someone tries to make us go to camp next summer, we can *really* run away."

All at once someone twisted my arm from behind and whispered so close to my ear that I could smell cheese breath. "Move it," said Earl.

"Yeah, move it," echoed Bubba Joe.

So I went where Earl pushed me, to the record-and-video department about thirty feet from the snack bar, mainly because I didn't want to create a scene right in the middle of the ZCMI department store, in case some kid like Rob Farrell from Bryant Junior High School happened to be watching. The two Spikeses and I stopped behind the rack of classical CDs, where there weren't any customers.

"You know what happens to eavesdropping finks?" Bubba Joe said.

I knew I was supposed to be scared, but I wasn't. I giggled.

That made Earl mad. He twisted my arm tighter. "You tell my mother where we were last month and you're dead meat."

"With ten broken toes," offered Bubba Joe.

"I'm not afraid of you," I said.

I wasn't, either. For the first time I realized that they were the ones who were afraid of me—that they'd been afraid of me all along. For the first time I realized that I'd always had the upper hand.

"I'll make a bargain with you," I offered. "I won't tell your mother where you were if you'll answer a few questions I need to know, like first of all, how you got into Mrs. Overfield's house."

Earl loosened his grip on me, and the two boys looked at each other and shrugged.

"I found her keys," said Bubba Joe.

"I know that," I said. "Where?"

"In her purse," said Earl.

"Where was her purse?" I insisted.

"In a garbage can a few blocks from here," said Bubba Joe. "We didn't have much money, so we started looking in garbage cans for good stuff. I found the best stuff, didn't I, Earl?"

Earl wriggled one of his bare feet in and out

of a thonged sandal. "I guess so."

"I found the purse with her house keys and her car keys and that paper that told Mrs. Over field's name and address and what planes she was going on. I found the best stuff," Bubba Joe repeated.

"Earl! Bubba Joe!" called their mother. "Where are you two anyway?"

"Right here," said Earl, just as if he were the sort of kid who always answered when grown-ups called.

"Come on now," said their mother. "I'm tired."

And the two of them followed after their mother and the other kids as obedient as the newly trained Thomas Jefferson.

Darci handed me a paper plate dripping with melted cheese. "Who were those boys you were talking to?"

"Oh, them? Just some kids I know."

"Tell me about the big one. He's *kee-yute!*"

It had never occurred to me before that Earl Spikes was anything besides a none-too-bright bully, but I guess I was pleased that Darci thought I knew a cute boy that she didn't.

"Oh, Earl!" I said with a wave of my hand in the air. Then I paused, thinking about his red hair. It wasn't really frizzy like the other Spikes kids' hair, just nice and curly. And for a guy our age, he had pretty broad shoulders. In my mind I could just see Brynne's and Jannalee's faces when Darci described the new guy I'd been keeping to myself. "Yeah, he's kind of cute. On a scale of one to ten, I guess he's maybe a seven."

"At least," gushed Darci. "At least."